WORLD CULTURAL
HERITAGE LIBRARY

I0554418

A VAGABONDIA SONGS

Bliss Carman Richard Hovey

PUBLISHED FIRST: *1894, 1896, 1900 London*
REPRINT 2013 ISBN: 1-4330-9599-8

A VAGABONDIA SONGS

by Bliss Carman Richard Hovey

CONTENTS

BLISS CARMAN

Born	William Bliss Carman April 15, 1861 Fredericton, New Brunswick
Died	June 8, 1929 (aged 68) New Canaan, Connecticut
Resting place	Fredericton, New Brunswick
Occupation	poet
Language	English
Nationality	Canadian
Citizenship	British subject
Education	U of New Brunswick, U of Edinburgh, Harvard U
Genres	poetry
Literary movement	Confederation Poets, The Song Fishermen
Notable work(s)	Low Tide on Grand Pré, Songs from Vagabondia, Sappho: 100 Lyrics
Notable award(s)	Lorne Pierce Medal, FRSC

Bliss Carman FRSC (April 15, 1861 – June 8, 1929) was a Canadian poet who lived most of his life in the United States, where he achieved international fame. He was acclaimed as Canada's poet laureate during his later years.

In Canada Carman is classed as one of the Confederation Poets, a group which also included Charles G.D. Roberts (his cousin), Archibald Lampman, and Duncan Campbell Scott. "Of the group, Carman had the surest lyric touch and achieved the widest international recognition. But unlike others, he never attempted to secure his income by novel writing, popular journalism, or non-literary employment. He remained a poet, supplementing his art with critical commentaries on literary ideas, philosophy, and aesthetics

LIFE

He was born **William Bliss Carman** in Fredericton, in the Maritime province of New Brunswick. "Bliss" was his mother's maiden name. He was the great grandson of United Empire Loyalists who fled to Nova Scotia after the American Revolution, settling in New Brunswick (then part of Nova Scotia). His literary roots run deep with an ancestry that includes a mother who was a descendant of Daniel Bliss of Concord, Massachusetts, the great-grandfather of Ralph Waldo Emerson. His sister married the botanist and historian William Francis Ganong. And on his mother's side he was a first cousin to Charles (later Sir Charles) G. D. Roberts.

Education and early career

Carman was educated at the Fredericton Collegiate School and the University of New Brunswick (UNB), from which he received a B.A. in 1881. At the Collegiate School he came under the influence of headmaster George Robert Parkin, who gave him a love of classical literature and introduced him to the poetry of Dante Gabriel Rossetti and Algernon Charles Swinburne. His first published poem was in the *UNB Monthly* in 1879. He then spent a year at Oxford and the University of Edinburgh (1882–1883), but returned home to receive his M.A. from UNB in 1884.

After the death of his father in January 1885 and his mother in February 1886, Carman enrolled in Harvard University (1886–

1887). At Harvard he moved in a literary circle that included American poet Richard Hovey, who would become his close friend and his collaborator on the successful *Vagabondia* poetry series. Their circle also included Herbert Copeland and F. Holland Day, who would later form the Boston publishing firm Copeland & Day that would launch *Vagabondia*.

After Harvard Carman briefly returned to Canada, but was back in Boston by February 1890. "Boston is one of the few places where my critical education and tastes could be of any use to me in earning money," he wrote. "New York and London are about the only other places." Unable to find employment in Boston, he moved to New York City and became literary editor of the *New York Independent* at the grand sum of $20/week. There he could help his Canadian friends get published, in the process "introducing Canadian poets to its readers." However, Carman was never a good fit at the semi-religious weekly, and he was summarily dismissed in 1892. "Brief stints would follow with *Current Literature, Cosmopolitan, The Chap-Book*, and *The Atlantic Monthly*, but after 1895 he would be strictly a contributor to the magazines and newspapers, never an editor in any department."

To make matters worse, Carman's first book of poetry, 1893's *Low Tide on Grand Pré*, was not a success; no Canadian company would publish it, and the U.S. edition stiffed when its publisher went bankrupt.

Literary success

At this low point, *Songs of Vagabondia,* the first Hovey-Carman collaboration, was published by Copeland & Day in 1894. It was an immediate success. "No one could have been more surprised at the tremendous popularity of these care-free celebrations (the first of the three collections went through seven rapid editions) than the young authors, Richard Hovey and Bliss Carman." *Songs of Vagabondia* would ultimately "go through sixteen printings (ranging from 500 to 1000 copies) over the next thirty years.

The three *Vagabondia* volumes that followed fell slightly short of that record, but each went through numerous printings. Carman and Hovey quickly found themselves with a cult following, especially among college students, who responded to the poetry's anti-materialistic themes, its celebration of individual freedom, and its glorification of comradeship."

The success of *Songs of Vagabondia* prompted another Boston firm, Stone & Kimball, to reissue *Low Tide...* and to hire Carman as the editor of its literary journal, *The Chapbook*. The next year, though, the editor's job went West (with Stone & Kimball) to Chicago, while Carman opted to remain in Boston.

"In Boston in 1895, he worked on a new poetry book, *Behind the Arras*, which he placed with a prominent Boston publisher (Lamson, Wolffe).... He published two more books of verse with Lamson, Wolffe." He also began writing a weekly column for the Boston *Evening Transcript*, which ran from 1895 to 1900.

In 1896 Carman met Mary Perry King, who became the greatest and longest-lasting female influence in his life. Mrs. King became his patron: "She put pence in his purse, and food in his mouth, when he struck bottom and, what is more, she often put a song on his lips when he despaired, and helped him sell it." According to Carman's roommate, Mitchell Kennerley, "On rare occasions they had intimate relations at 10 E. 16 which they always advised me of by leaving a bunch of violets — Mary Perry's favorite flower — on the pillow of my bed." If he knew of the latter, Dr. King did not object: "He even supported her involvement in the career of Bliss Carman to the extent that the situation developed into something close to a *ménage à trois*" with the Kings.

Through Mrs. King's influence Carman became an advocate of 'unitrinianism,' a philosophy which "drew on the theories of François-Alexandre-Nicolas-Chéri Delsarte to develop a strategy of mind-body-spirit harmonization aimed at undoing the physical, psychological, and spiritual damage caused by urban modernity." This shared belief created a bond between Mrs. King and Carman but estranged him somewhat from his former friends.

In 1899 Lamson, Wolffe was taken over by the Boston firm of Small, Maynard & Co., who had also acquired the rights to *Low Tide...* "The rights to all Carman's books were now held by one publisher and, in lieu of earnings, Carman took a financial stake in the company. When Small, Maynard failed in 1903, Carman lost all his assets."

Down but not out, Carman signed with another Boston company, L.C. Page, and began to churn out new work. Page published seven books of new Carman poetry between 1902 and 1905.

As well, the firm released three books based on Carman's *Transcript* columns, and a prose work on unitrinianism, *The Making of Personality*, that he'd written with Mrs. King. "Page also helped Carman rescue his 'dream project,' a deluxe edition of his collected poetry to 1903.... Page acquired distribution rights with the stipulation that the book be sold privately, by subscription. The project failed; Carman was deeply disappointed and became disenchanted with Page, whose grip on Carman's copyrights would prevent the publication of another collected edition during Carman's lifetime."

Carman also picked up some needed cash in 1904 as editor-in-chief of the 10-volume project, The World's Best Poetry.

Later years

After 1908 Carman lived near the Kings' New Canaan, Connecticut, estate, "Sunshine", or in the summer in a cabin near their summer home in the Catskills, "Moonshine." Between 1908 and 1920, literary taste began to shift, and his fortunes and health declined.

"Although not a political activist, Carman during the First World War was a member of the Vigilantes, who supported American entry into the conflict on the Allied side."

By 1920, Carman was impoverished and recovering from a near-fatal attack of tuberculosis. That year he revisited Canada and "began the first of a series of successful and relatively lucrative reading tours, discovering 'there is nothing worth talking of in book sales compared with reading.'" "'Breathless attention, crowded halls, and a strange, profound enthusiasm such as I never guessed could be,' he reported to a friend. 'And good thrifty money too. Think of it! An entirely new life for me, and I am the most surprised person in Canada.'"

Carmen was feted at "a dinner held by the newly-formed Canadian Authors' Association at the Ritz Carlton Hotel in

Montreal on 28 October 1921 where he was crowned Canada's Poet Laureate with a wreath of maple leaves."

The tours of Canada continued, and by 1925 Carman had finally acquired a Canadian publisher. "McClelland & Stewart (Toronto) issued a collection of selected earlier verses and became his main publisher. They benefited from Carman's popularity and his revered position in Canadian literature, but no one could convince L.C. Page to relinquish its copyrights. An edition of collected poetry was published only after Carman's death, due greatly to the persistence of his literary executor, Lorne Pierce."

During the 1920s, Carman was a member of the Halifax literary and social set, The Song Fishermen. In 1927 he edited *The Oxford Book of American Verse*.

Carman died of a brain hemorrhage at the age of 68 in New Canaan, and was cremated in New Canaan. "It took two months, and the influence of New Brunswick's Premier J.B.M. Baxter and Canadian Prime Minister W.L.M. King, for Carman's ashes to be returned to Fredericton."

"His ashes were buried in Forest Hill Cemetery, Fredericton, and a national memorial service was held at the Anglican cathedral there." Twenty-five years later, on May 13, 1954, a scarlet maple tree was planted at his gravesite, to grant his request in his 1892 poem "The Grave-Tree":

> Let me have a scarlet maple
>
> For the grave-tree at my head,
>
> With the quiet sun behind it,
>
> In the years when I am dead.

WRITING

Low Tide on Grand Pré

As a student at Harvard, Carman "was heavily influenced by Josiah Royce, whose spiritualistic idealism, combined with the transcendentalism of Ralph Waldo Emerson, lies centrally in the background of his first major poem, "Low Tide on Grand Pré" written in the summer and winter of 1886." "Low Tide..." was published in the Spring, 1887 *Atlantic Monthly*, giving Carman a literary reputation while still at Harvard. It was also included in the 1889 anthology, *Songs of the Great Dominion.*

Literary critic Desmond Pacey considered "Low Tide..." to be "the most nearly perfect single poem to come out of Canada. It will withstand any amount of critical scrutiny."

"Low Tide..." served as the title poem for Carman's first book. "The poems in this volume have been collected with reference to their similarity of tone," Carman wrote in his preface; a nostalgic tone of pervading loss and melancholy. Three outstanding examples are "The Eavesdropper," "In Apple Time" and "Wayfaring." However, "none can equal the artistry of the title poem. What is more, although Carman would publish over thirty other volumes during his lifetime, none of them contains anything that surpasses this poem he wrote when he was barely twenty-five years old."

Vagabondia

Carmen rose to prominence in the 1890s, a decade the poetry of which anthologist Louis Untermeyer has called marked by "a cheerless evasion, a humorous unconcern; its most representative craftsmen were, with four exceptions, the writers of light verse."

The first two of those four exceptions were Richard Hovey and Bliss Carman. For Untermeyer: "The poetry of this period ... is dead because it detached itself from the world.... But ... revolt openly declared itself with the publication of **Songs from Vagabondia** (1894), **More Songs from Vagabondia** (1896), and **Last Songs from Vagabondia** (1900).... It was the heartiness, the gypsy jollity, the rush of high spirits, that conquered. Readers of the *Vagabondia* books were swept along by their speed faster than by their philosophy."

Even modernists loved *Vagabondia*. In the "October, 1912 issue of the *London Poetry Review,* Ezra Pound noted that he had 'greatly enjoyed *The Songs of Vagabondia* by Mr. Bliss Carman and the late Richard Hovey.'"

Carman's most famous poem from the first volume is arguably "The Joys of the Open Road." *More Songs...* contains "A Vagabond Song," once familiar to a generation of Canadians. "Canadian youngsters who were in grade seven anytime between the mid-1930s and the 1950s were probably exposed to ... 'A Vagabond Song' [which] appeared in *The Canada Book of Prose and Verse, Book One*, the school reader that was used in nearly every province" (and was edited by Lorne Pierce).

In 1912 Carman would publish **Echoes from Vagabondia** as a solo work. (Hovey had died in 1900). More of a remembrance book than part of the set, it has a distinct elegiac tone. It contains the lyric "The Flute of Spring."

Behind the Arras

With *Behind the Arras* (1895), Carman continued his practice of "bringing together poems that were 'in the same key.' Whereas *Low Tide on Grand Pré* is elegiacal and melancholy, *Songs from Vagabondia* is mostly light and jaunty, while *Behind the Arras* is philosophical and heavy."

"Behind the Arras" the poem is a long meditation that uses the speaker's house and its many rooms as a symbol of life and its choices. The poem does not succeed: "there are so many asides that the allegory is lost along with any point the poet hoped to make."

Ballad of Lost Haven

In keeping with the "same key" idea, Carman's *Ballad of Lost Haven* (1897) was a collection of poetry about the sea. Its notable poems include the macabre sea shanty, "The Gravedigger."

By the Aurelian Wall

"By the Aurelian Wall" is Carman's elegy to John Keats. It served as the title poem of his 1898 collection, a book of formal elegies.

In the last poem in the book, "The Grave-Tree," Carman writes about his own death.

The Pipes of Pan

"Pan, the goat-god, traditionally associated with poetry and with the fusion of the earthly and the divine, becomes Carman's organizing symbol in the five volumes issued between 1902 and 1905" under the above title.

Under the influence of Mrs. King, Carman had begun to write in both prose and poetry about the ideas of 'unitrinianism,' "a strategy of mind-body-spirit harmonization aimed at undoing the physical, psychological, and spiritual damage caused by urban modernity ... therapeutic ideas [which] resulted in the five volumes of verse assembled in *Pipes of Pan*." The *Dictionary of Canadian Biography (DCB)* calls the series "a collection that contains many superb lyrics but, overall, evinces the dangers of a soporific aesthetic."

The 'superb lyrics' include the much-anthologized "The Dead Faun" from Volume I, *From the Book of Myths*; "From the Green Book of the Bards", the title poem of Volume II; "Lord of My Heart's Elation" from the same volume; and many of the erotic poems of Volume III, *Songs of the Sea Children* (such as LIX ("I loved you when the tide of prayer"). As a whole, though, the Pan series shows (perhaps more than any other work) the truth of Northrop Frye's 1954 observation that Carman "badly needs a skillful and sympathetic selection."

Sappho: One Hundred Lyrics

There were no such problems with Carman's next book. Perhaps because of the underlying concept, *Sappho: One Hundred Lyrics* (1904) has a structure and unity that helps make it what has been called Carman's "finest volume of poetry."

Sappho was an Ancient Greek poet from the island of Lesbos, who was included in the Greek canon of nine lyric poets. Most of her poetry, which was well-known and greatly admired throughout antiquity, has been lost, but her reputation has endured, supported by the surviving fragments of some of her poems.

Carman's method, as Charles G.D. Roberts saw it in his Introduction to the book,"apparently, has been to imagine each lost lyric as discovered, and then to translate it; for the indefinable flavor of the translation is maintained throughout, though accompanied by the fluidity and freedom of purely original work." It was a daunting task, as Roberts admits: "It is as if a sculptor of to-day were to set himself, with reverence, and trained craftsmanship, and studious familiarity with the spirit, technique, and atmosphere of his subject, to restore some statues of Polyclitus or Praxiteles of which he had but a broken arm, a foot, a knee, a finger upon which to build." Yet, on the whole, Carman succeeded.

"Written more or less contemporaneously with the love poems in *Songs of the Sea Children*, the Sappho reconstructions continue the amorous theme from a feminine point of view. Nevertheless, the feelings ascribed to Sappho are pure Carman in their sensitive and elegiac melancholy."

Virtually all of the lyrics are of high quality; some often-quoted are XXIII ("I loved thee, Atthis, in the long ago,"), LIV ("How soon will all my lovely days be over"), LXXIV ("If death be good"), LXXXII ("Over the roofs the honey-coloured moon")

"Next to *Low Tide on Grand Pré*, *Sappho: One Hundred Lyrics* seems to be the collection that continues to find the most favour among Carman's critics. D.M.R. Bentley, for example, calls it 'undoubtedly one of the most attractive, engaging and satisfying works of any of the Confederation poets.'" Bentley argued that "the brief, crisp lyrics of the *Sappho* volume almost certainly contributed to the aesthetic and practice of Imagism.

LATER WORK

In his review of 1954's *Selected Poems of Bliss Carman*, literary critic Northrop Frye compared Carman and the other Confederation Poets to the Group of Seven: "Like the later painters, these poets were lyrical in tone and romantic in attitude; like the painters, they sought for the most part uninhabited landscape." But Frye added: "The lyrical response to landscape is by itself, however, a kind of emotional photography, and like other forms of photography is occasional and epigrammatic.... Hence the lyric poet, after he has run his gamut of impressions, must die young, develop a more intellectualized attitude, or start repeating himself. Carman's meeting of this challenge was only partly successful."

It is true that Carman had begun to repeat himself after *Sappho*. "Much of Carman's writing in poetry and prose during the decade preceding World War I is as repetitive as the title of *Echoes from Vagabondia* (1912) intimates" says the *DCB*. What had made his poetry so remarkable at the beginning – that every new book was completely new – was gone.

However, Carman's career was by no means over. He "published four other collections of new poetry during his lifetime and two more were ready for publication at the time of his death: **The Rough Rider, and Other Poems** (1908), **A Painter's Holiday, and Other Poems** (1911), **April Airs** (1916), **Far Horizons** (1925), **Sanctuary** (1929), and **Wild Garden** (1929). James Cappon's comment on *Far Horizons* applies almost equally to the other five volumes: 'There is nothing new in its poetic quality which has the sweet sadness of age rehearsing old tunes with an art which is now very smooth though with less vivacity than it used to have.'"

Not only did Carman continue to write, but he continued to write fine poems: poems such as "The Old Grey Wall" (*April Airs*), the Wilfred Campbell-ish "Rivers of Canada" (*Far Horizons*), "The Ghost-yard of the Goldenrod" and "The Ships of Saint John" (*Later Poems*, 1926), and "The Winter Scene" (*Sanctuary: The "Sunshine House" sonnets*). The best of these have the same nostalgic air of melancholy and loss with which Carman began in "Low Tide...," but now even more poignant as the poet approached his own death.

RECOGNITION

In 1906 Carman received honorary degrees from UNB and McGill University.

Carman was elected a corresponding Fellow of the Royal Society of Canada in 1925. The Society awarded him its Lorne Pierce Gold Medal in 1928.

He was awarded a medal from the American Academy of Arts and Letters in 1929.

Carman is honored by a sculpture erected on the UNB campus in 1947, which portrays him with fellow poets Sir Charles G.D. Roberts and Francis Joseph Sherman

There is a middle school named after him in Fredericton, New Brunswick. There is also a school named after him in Toronto, Ontario.

"Bliss Carman Heights" (an extension of the Skyline Acres subdivision) is a subdivision located in Fredericton, New Brunswick overlooking the Saint John River. It consists of Essex Street, Gloucester Crescent, Reading Street, Ascot Court, and Ascot Drive. An extension of the Bliss Carman Heights subdivision is named "Poet's Hill" and consists of Bliss Carman Drive, Poets Lane and Windflower Court (named for one of Carman's poems of the same name).

RICHARD HOVEY

Richard Hovey (May 4, 1864 – February 24, 1900) was an American poet. Graduating from Dartmouth College in 1885, he is known in part for penning the school Alma Mater, *Men of Dartmouth*.

Hovey was born in Normal, Illinois, the son of Major General Charles Edward Hovey and Harriet Spofford Hovey. He grew up in North Amherst, Massachusetts, and in Washington, D.C., before attending Dartmouth. His first volume of poems was privately published in 1880.

He collaborated with Canadian poet Bliss Carman on three volumes of "tramp" verse: *Songs from Vagabondia* (1894), *More Songs from Vagabondia* (1896), and *Last Songs from Vagabondia* (1900), the last being published after Hovey's death.

Some twenty-nine poets have attempted to write sequels for Byron's *Don Juan*. Hovey was one of them. Samuel Chew praised Hovey's "Canto XVII" in his book *To the End of the Trail*. "This is one of the most convincing reproductions of the spirit and movement of Byron's verse that I have ever come across. It is supposed to be written by Byron in Hades. The poet refuses to take up the poem at the point at which Death had cut him short.—

> *Southey's forgotten; so is Castlereagh;*
> *But there are fools and scoundrels still today.*

In the sequel we hear nothing of Juan; the satire is expended upon current affairs. Byron is full of curiosity as to events on earth:

> *I've such a next-day's thirst for information,*
> *I'd even be content to read the Nation.*

He died after undergoing minor abdominal surgery in 1900.

SELECTED POEMS

SeaGypsy
When We Are Dead
John Keats
To a Friend
Philosophy
The Old Pine
In Memoriam
Squab Flights
Kronos
College Days
Dante Gabriel Rossetti
The South

SONGS FROM VAGABONDIA

Bliss Carman Richard Hovey

Boston Copeland and Day
London
Elkin Mathews and John Lane

MDCCCXCIV

1894, BY BLISS CARMAN AND RICHARD HOVEY.

To H.F.W., for debts of love unpaid,
Her boys inscribe this book that they have made.

VAGABONDIA.

Off with the fetters
That chafe and restrain!
Off with the chain!
Here Art and Letters,
Music and wine,
And Myrtle and Wanda,
The winsome witches,
Blithely combine.
Here are true riches,
Here is Golconda,
Here are the Indies,
Here we are free—
Free as the wind is,
Free, as the sea.
Free!

Houp-la!

What have we
To do with the way
Of the Pharisee?
We go or we stay
At our own sweet will;
We think as we say,
And we say or keep still
At our own sweet will,
At our own sweet will.

Here we are free
To be good or bad,
Sane or mad,
Merry or grim
As the mood may be,—
Free as the whim
Of a spook on a spree,—
Free to be oddities,
Not mere commodities,
Stupid and salable,
Wholly available,
Ranged upon shelves;
Each with his puny form
In the same uniform,
Cramped and disabled;
We are not labelled,

We are ourselves.

Here is the real,
Here the ideal;
Laughable hardship
Met and forgot,
Glory of bardship—
World's bloom and world's blot;
The shock and the jostle,
The mock and the push,
But hearts like the throstle
A-joy in the bush;
Wits that would merrily
Laugh away wrong,
Throats that would verily
Melt Hell in Song.

What though the dimes be
Elusive as rhymes be,
And Bessie, with finger
Uplifted, is warning
That breakfast next morning
(A subject she's scorning)
Is mighty uncertain!

What care we? Linger
A moment to kiss—
No time's amiss
To a vagabond's ardor—
Thee finish the larder
And pull down the curtain.

Unless ere the kiss come,
Black Richard or Bliss come,
Or Tom with a flagon,
Or Karl with a jag on—
Then up and after
The joy of the night
With the hounds of laughter
To follow the flight
Of the fox-foot hours
That double and run
Through brakes and bowers
Of folly and fun.

With the comrade heart
For a moment's play,
And the comrade heart
For a heavier day,
And the comrade heart
Forever and aye.

For the joy of wine
Is not for long;
And the joy of song
Is a dream of shine;
But the comrade heart
Shall outlast art
And a woman's love
The fame thereof.

But wine for a sign
Of the love we bring!
And song for an oath
That Love is king!
And both, and both
For his worshipping!

Then up and away
Till the break of day,
With a heart that's merry,
And a Tom-and-Jerry,
And a derry-down-derry—
What's that you say.
You highly respectable
Buyers and sellers?
We should be decenter?
Not as we please inter
Custom, frugality,
Use and morality
In the delectable
Depths of wine-cellars?

Midnights of revel,
And noondays of song!
Is it so wrong?
Go to the Devil!

I tell you that we,
While you are smirking

And lying and shirking
life's duty of duties,
Honest sincerity,
We are in verity
Free!
Free to rejoice

In blisses and beauties!
Free as the voice
Of the wind as it passes!
Free as the bird
In the weft of the grasses!
Free as the word
Of the sun to the sea—
Free!

A WAIF.

Do you know what it is to be vagrant born?
A waif is only a waif. And so,
For another idle hour I sit,
In large content while the fire burns low.

I gossip here to my crony heart
Of the day just over, and count it one
Of the royal elemental days,
Though its dreams were few and its deeds were none.

Outside, the winter; inside, the warmth
And a sweet oblivion of turmoil. Why?
All for a gentle girlish hand
With its warm and lingering good-bye.

THE JOYS OF THE ROAD.

Now the joys of the road are chiefly these:
A crimson touch on the hard-wood trees;

A vagrant's morning wide and blue,
In early fall when the wind walks, too;

A shadowy highway cool and brown,
Alluring up and enticing down

From rippled water to dappled swamp,
From purple glory to scarlet pomp;

The outward eye, the quiet will,
And the striding heart from hill to hill;

The tempter apple over the fence;
The cobweb bloom on the yellow quince;

The palish asters along the wood,—
A lyric touch of the solitude;

An open hand, an easy shoe.
And a hope to make the day go through,—

Another to sleep with, and a third
To wake me up at the voice of a bird;

The resonant far-listening morn,
And the hoarse whisper of the corn;

The crickets mourning their comrades lost,
In the night's retreat from the gathering frost;

(Or is it their slogan, plaintive and shrill,
As they beat on their corselets, valiant still?)

A hunger fit for the kings of the sea,
And a loaf of bread for Dickon and me;

A thirst like that of the Thirsty Sword,
And a jug of cider on the board;

An idle noon, a bubbling spring,
The sea in the pine-tops murmuring;

A scrap of gossip at the ferry;
A comrade neither glum nor merry,

Asking nothing, revealing naught,
But minting his words from a fund of thought,

A keeper of silence eloquent,
Needy, yet royally well content,

Of the mettled breed, yet abhorring strife,
And full of the mellow juice of life;

A taster of wine, with an eye for a maid,
Never too bold, and never afraid,

Never heart-whole, never heart-sick,
(These are the things I worship in Dick)

No fidget and no reformer, just
A calm observer of ought and must,

A lover of books, but a reader of man,
No cynic and no charlatan,

Who never defers and never demands,
But, smiling, takes the world in his hands,—

Seeing it good as when God first saw
And gave it the weight of his will for law.

And O the joy that is never won,
But follows and follows the journeying sun,

By marsh and tide, by meadow and stream,
A will-o'-the-wind, a light-o'-dream,

Delusion afar, delight anear,
From morrow to morrow, from year to year,

A jack-o'-lantern, a fairy fire,
A dare, a bliss, and a desire!

The racy smell of the forest loam,
When the stealthy, sad-heart leaves go home;

(O leaves, O leaves, I am one with you,
Of the mould and the sun and the wind and the dew!)

The broad gold wake of the afternoon;
The silent fleck of the cold new moon;

The sound of the hollow sea's release
From stormy tumult to starry peace;

With only another league to wend;
And two brown arms at the journey's end!

These are the joys of the open road—
For him who travels without a load.

EVENING ON THE POTOMAC.

The fervid breath of our flushed Southern May
Is sweet upon the city's throat and lips,
As a lover's whose tired arm slips
Listlessly over the shoulder of a queen.

Far away
The river melts in the unseen.
Oh, beautiful Girl-City, how she dips
Her feet in the stream
With a touch that is half a kiss and half a dream!
Her face is very fair,
With flowers for smiles and sunlight in her hair.

My westland flower-town, how serene she is!
Here on this hill from which I look at her,
All is still as if a worshipper
Left at some shrine his offering.

Soft winds kiss
My cheek with a slow lingering.
A luring whisper where the laurels stir
Wiles my heart back to woodland-ward again.

But lo,
Across the sky the sunset couriers run,
And I remain
To watch the imperial pageant of the Sun
Mock me, an impotent Cortez here below,
With splendors of its vaster Mexico.

O Eldorado of the templed clouds!
O golden city of the western sky!
Not like the Spaniard would I storm thy gates;
Not like the babe stretch chubby hands and cry

To have thee for a toy; but far from crowds,
Like my Faun brother in the ferny glen,
Peer from the wood's edge while thy glory waits,
And in the darkening thickets plunge again.

SPRING SONG.

Make me over, mother April,
When the sap begins to stir!
When thy flowery hand delivers
All the mountain-prisoned rivers,
And thy great heart beats and quivers,
To revive the days that were,
Make me over, mother April,
When the sap begins to stir!

Take my dust and all my dreaming,
Count my heart-beats one by one,
Send them where the winters perish;
Then some golden noon recherish
And restore them in the sun,
Flower and scent and dust and dreaming,
With their heart-beats every one!

Set me in the urge and tide-drift
Of the streaming hosts a-wing!
Breast of scarlet, throat of yellow,
Raucous challenge, wooings mellow—
Every migrant is my fellow,
Making northward with the spring.
Loose me in the urge and tide-drift
Of the streaming hosts a-wing!

Shrilling pipe or fluting whistle,
In the valleys come again;
Fife of frog and call of tree-toad,
All my brothers, five or three-toed,
With their revel no more vetoed,
Making music in the rain;
Shrilling pipe or fluting whistle,
In the valleys come again.

Make me of thy seed to-morrow,
When the sap begins to stir!
Tawny light-foot, sleepy bruin,
Bright-eyes in the orchard ruin,
Gnarl the good life goes askew in,
Whiskey-jack, or tanager,—
Make me anything to-morrow,
When the sap begins to stir!

Make me even (How do I know?)
Like my friend the gargoyle there;
It may be the heart within him
Swells that doltish hands should pin him
Fixed forever in mid-air.
Make me even sport for swallows,
Like the soaring gargoyle there!

Give me the old clue to follow,
Through the labyrinth of night!
Clod of clay with heart of fire,
Things that burrow and aspire,
With the vanishing desire,
For the perishing delight,—
Only the old clue to follow,
Through the labyrinth of night!

Make me over, mother April,
When the sap begins to stir!
Fashion me from swamp or meadow,
Garden plot or ferny shadow,
Hyacinth or humble burr!
Make me over, mother April,
When the sap begins to stir!

Let me hear the far, low summons,
When the silver winds return;
Rills that run and streams that stammer,
Goldenwing with his loud hammer,
Icy brooks that brawl and clamor,
Where the Indian willows burn;
Let me hearken to the calling,
When the silver winds return,

Till recurring and recurring,
Long since wandered and come back,
Like a whim of Grieg's or Gounod's,
This same self, bird, bud, or Bluenose,
Some day I may capture (Who knows?)
Just the one last joy I lack,
Waking to the far new summons,
When the old spring winds come back.

For I have no choice of being,
When the sap begins to climb,—

Strong insistence, sweet intrusion,
Vasts and verges of illusion,—
So I win, to time's confusion,
The one perfect pearl of time,
Joy and joy and joy forever,
Till the sap forgets to climb!

Make me over in the morning
From the rag-bag of the world!
Scraps of dream and duds of daring,
Home-brought stuff from far sea-faring,
Faded colors once so flaring,
Shreds of banners long since furled!
Hues of ash and glints of glory,
In the rag-bag of the world!

Let me taste the old immortal
Indolence of life once more;
Not recalling nor foreseeing,
Let the great slow joys of being
Well my heart through as of yore!
Let me taste the old immortal
Indolence of life once more!

Give me the old drink for rapture,
The delirium to drain,
All my fellows drank in plenty
At the Three Score Inns and Twenty
From the mountains to the main!
Give me the old drink for rapture,
The delirium to drain!

Only make me over, April,
When the sap begins to stir!
Make me man or make me woman,
Make me oaf or ape or human,
Cup of flower or cone of fir;
Make me anything but neuter
When the sap begins to stir!

THE FAUN. A FRAGMENT.

I will go out to grass with that old King,
For I am weary of clothes and cooks.
I long to lie along the banks of brooks,

And watch the boughs above me sway and swing.
Come, I will pluck off custom's livery,
Nor longer be a lackey to old Time.
Time shall serve me, and at my feet shall fling
The spoil of listless minutes. I shall climb
The wild trees for my food, and run
Through dale and upland as a fox runs free,
Laugh for cool joy and sleep i' the warm sun,
And men will call me mad, like that old King.

For I am woodland-natured, and have made
Dryads my bedfellows,
And I have played
With the sleek Naiads in the splash of pools
And made a mock of gowned and trousered fools.
Helen, none knows
Better than thou how like a Faun I strayed.
And I am half Faun now, and my heart goes
Out to the forest and the crack of twigs,
The drip of wet leaves and the low soft laughter
Of brooks that chuckle o'er old mossy jests
And say them over to themselves, the nests
Of squirrels and the holes the chipmunk digs,
Where through the branches the slant rays
Dapple with sunlight the leaf-matted ground,
And the wind comes with blown vesture rustling after,
And through the woven lattice of crisp sound
A bird's song lightens like a maiden's face.

O wildwood Helen, let them strive and fret,
Those goggled men with their dissecting-knives!

Let them in charnel-houses pass their lives
And seek in death life's secret! And let
Those hard-faced worldlings prematurely old
Gnaw their thin lips with vain desire to get
Portia's fair fame or Lesbia's carcanet,
Or crown of Caesar or Catullus,
Apicius' lampreys or Crassus' gold!
For these consider many things—but yet
By land nor sea
They shall not find the way to Arcady,
The old home of the awful heart-dear Mother,
Whereto child-dreams and long rememberings lull us,
Far from the cares that overlay and smother

The memories of old woodland out-door mirth
In the dim first life-burst centuries ago,
The sense of the freedom and nearness of Earth—
Nay, this they shall not know;
For who goes thither,
Leaves all the cark and clutch of his soul behind,
The doves defiled and the serpents shrined,
The hates that wax and the hopes that wither;
Nor does he journey, seeking where it be,
But wakes and finds himself in Arcady.

Hist! there's a stir in the brush.
Was it a face through the leaves?
Back of the laurels a skurry and rush
Hillward, then silence except for the thrush
That throws one song from the dark of the bush
And is gone; and I plunge in the wood, and the swift soul
cleaves
Through the swirl and the flow of the leaves,
As a swimmer stands with his white limbs bare to the sun
For the space that a breath is held, and drops in the sea;
And the undulant woodland folds round me, intimate, fluctuant,
free,
Like the clasp and the cling of waters, and the reach and the
effort is done,—
There is only the glory of living, exultant to be.

O goodly damp smell of the ground!
O rough sweet bark of the trees!
O clear sharp cracklings of sound!
O life that's a-thrill and a-bound
With the vigor of boyhood and morning, and the noontide's
rapture of ease!
Was there ever a weary heart in the world?
A lag in the body's urge or a flag of the spirit's wings?
Did a man's heart ever break
For a lost hope's sake?
For here there is lilt in the quiet and calm in the quiver of
things.
Ay, this old oak, gray-grown and knurled,
Solemn and sturdy and big,
Is as young of heart, as alert and elate in his rest,
As the nuthatch there that clings to the tip of the twig
And scolds at the wind that it buffets too rudely its nest.

Oh, what is it breathes in the air?
Oh, what is it touches my cheek?
There's a sense of a presence that lurks in the branches.
But where?
Is it far, is it far to seek?

A ROVER'S SONG.

Snowdrift of the mountains,
Spindrift of the sea,
We who down the border
Rove from gloom to glee,—

Snowdrift of the mountains,
Spindrift of the sea,
There be no such gypsies
Over earth as we.

Snowdrift of the mountains,
Spindrift of the sea,
Let us part the treasure
Of the world in three.

Snowdrift of the mountains,
Spindrift of the sea,
You shall keep your kingdoms;
Joscelyn for me!

DOWN THE SONGO.

I.

Floating!
Floating—and all the stillness waits
And listens at the ivory gates,
Full of a dim uncertain presage
Of some strange, undelivered message.
There is no sound save from the bush
The alto of the shy wood-thrush,
And ever and anon the dip
Of a lazy oar.

The rhythmic drowsiness keeps time
To hazy subtleties of rhyme
That seem to slip
Through the lulled soul to seek the sleepy shore.

The idle clouds go floating by;
Above us sky, beneath us sky;
The sun shines on us as we lie
Floating.

It is a dream.
It is a dream, my love; see how
The ripples quiver at the prow,
And all the long reflections shake
Unsteadily beneath the lake.
The mists about the uplands show
Dim violet towers that come and go.
Phantasmagoric palaces
Rise trembling there,
As though one breath of waking weather
Would crash their airy walls together
With sudden stress,
While silent detonations shook the air—
Vast fabrics toppling to the ground
And vanishing without a sound.
Ah, love, these are not what we deem;
It is a dream.

II.

Let us dream on, then,——dream and die
Ere the dream pass.
Let us for once, like idle flowers,
Let slip the unregarded hours,
Like the wise flowers that lie
Unfretted by a feeble thought,
Future and past alike forgot,
Drinking the dew contentedly
In the cool grass.

III.

Look yonder where the clouds float; could we glide
As they, across the sky's blue shoreless tide,
What better were it than to dream
Across yon lake and into this still stream?

IV.

Trees and a glimpse of sky!

And the slow river, quiet as a pool!
And thou and I—and thou and I—
Kiss me! How soft the air is and how cool!

THE WANDER-LOVERS.

Down the world with Marna!
That's the life for me!
Wandering with the wandering wind,
Vagabond and unconfined!
Roving with the roving rain
Its unboundaried domain!
Kith and kin of wander-kind,
Children of the sea!

Petrels of the sea-drift!
Swallows of the lea!
Arabs of the whole wide girth
Of the wind-encircled earth!
In all climes we pitch our tents,
Cronies of the elements,
With the secret lords of birth
Intimate and free.

All the seaboard knows us
From Fundy to the Keys;
Every bend and every creek
Of abundant Chesapeake;
Ardise hills and Newport coves
And the far-off orange groves,
Where Floridian oceans break,
Tropic tiger seas.

Down the world with Marna,
Tarrying there and here!
Just as much at home in Spain
As in Tangier or Touraine!
Shakespeare's Avon knows us well,
And the crags of Neufchâtel;
And the ancient Nile is fain
Of our coming near.

Down the world with Marna,
Daughter of the air!
Marna of the subtle grace,
And the vision in her face!

Moving in the measures trod
By the angels before God!
With her sky-blue eyes amaze
And her sea-blue hair!

Marna with the trees' life
In her veins a-stir!
Marna of the aspen heart
Where the sudden quivers start!
Quick-responsive, subtle, wild!
Artless as an artless child,
Spite of all her reach of art!
Oh, to roam with her!

Marna with the wind's will,
Daughter of the sea!
Marna of the quick disdain,
Starting at the dream of stain!
At a smile with love aglow,
At a frown a statued woe,
Standing pinnacled in pain
Till a kiss sets free!

Down the world with Marna,
Daughter of the fire!
Marna of the deathless hope,
Still alert to win new scope
Where the wings of life may spread
For a flight unhazarded!
Dreaming of the speech to cope
With the heart's desire!

Marna of the far quest
After the divine!
Striving ever for some goal
Past the blunder-god's control!
Dreaming of potential years
When no day shall dawn in fears!
That's the Marna of my soul,
Wander-bride of mine!

DISCOVERY.

When the bugler morn shall wind his horn,
And we wake to the wild to be,
Shall we open our eyes on the selfsame skies

And stare at the selfsame sea?
O new, new day! though you bring no stay
To the strain of the sameness grim,
You are new, new, new—new through and through,
And strange as a lawless dream.

Will the driftwood float by the lonely boat
And our prisoner hearts unbar,
As it tells of the strand of an unseen land
That lies not far, not far?
O new, new hope! O sweep and scope
Of the glad, unlying sea!
You are new, new, new—with the promise true
Of the dreamland isles to be.

Will the land-birds fly across the sky,
Though the land is not to see?
Have they dipped and passed in the sea-line vast?
Have we left the land a-lee?
O new despair! I though the hopeless air
Grow foul with the calm and grieves,
You are new, new, new—and we cleave to you
As a soul to its freedom cleaves.

Does the falling night hide fiends to fight
And phantoms to affray?
What demons lurk in the grisly mirk,
As the night-watch waits for day?
O strange new gloom! we await the doom,
And what doom none may deem;
But it's new, new, new—and we'll sail it through,
While the mocking sea-gulls scream.

A light, a light, in the dead of night,
That lifts and sinks in the waves!
What folk are they who have kindled its ray,—
Men or the ghouls of graves?
O new, new fear! near, near and near,
And you bear us weal or woe!
But you're new, new, new—so a cheer for you!
And onward—friend or foe!

Shall the lookout call from the foretop tall,
"Land, land!" with a maddened scream,
And the crew in glee from the taffrail see

Where the island palm-trees dream?
New heart, new eyes! For the morning skies
Are a-chant with their green and gold!
New, new, new, new—new through and through!
New, new till the dawn is old!

A MORE ANCIENT MARINER.

The swarthy bee is a buccaneer,
A burly velveted rover,
Who loves the booming wind in his ear
As he sails the seas of clover.

A waif of the goblin pirate crew,
With not a soul to deplore him,
He steers for the open verge of blue
With the filmy world before him.

His flimsy sails abroad on the wind
Are shivered with fairy thunder;
On a line that sings to the light of his wings
He makes for the lands of wonder.

He harries the ports of the Hollyhocks,
And levies on poor Sweetbrier;
He drinks the whitest wine of Phlox,
And the Rose is his desire.

He hangs in the Willows a night and a day;
He rifles the Buckwheat patches;
Then battens his store of pelf galore
Under the tautest hatches.

He woos the Poppy and weds the Peach,
Inveigles Daffodilly,
And then like a tramp abandons each
For the gorgeous Canada Lily.

There's not a soul in the garden world
But wishes the day were shorter,
When Mariner B. puts out to sea
With the wind in the proper quarter.

Or, so they say! But I have my doubts;
For the flowers are only human,
And the valor and gold of a vagrant bold

Were always dear to woman.

He dares to boast, along the coast,
The beauty of Highland Heather,—
How he and she, with night on the sea,
Lay out on the hills together.

He pilfers from every port of the wind,
From April to golden autumn;
But the thieving ways of his mortal days
Are those his mother taught him.

His morals are mixed, but his will is fixed;
He prospers after his kind,
And follows an instinct, compass-sure,
The philosophers call blind.

And that is why, when he comes to die,
He'll have an easier sentence
Than some one I know who thinks just so,
And then leaves room for repentance.

He never could box the compass round;
He doesn't know port from starboard;
But he knows the gates of the Sundown Straits,
Where the choicest goods are harbored.

He never could see the Rule of Three,
But he knows a rule of thumb
Better than Euclid's, better than yours,
Or the teachers' yet to come.

He knows the smell of the hydromel
As if two and two were five;
And hides it away for a year and a day
In his own hexagonal hive.

Out in the day, hap-hazard, alone,
Booms the old vagrant hummer,
With only his whim to pilot him
Through the splendid vast of summer.

He steers and steers on the slant of the gale,
Like the fiend or Vanderdecken;
And there's never an unknown course to sail

But his crazy log can reckon.

He drones along with his rough sea-song
And the throat of a salty tar,
This devil-may-care, till he makes his lair
By the light of a yellow star.

He looks like a gentleman, lives like a lord,
And works like a Trojan hero;
Then loafs all winter upon his hoard,
With the mercury at zero.

A SONG BY THE SHORE.

"Lose and love" is love's first art;
So it was with thee and me,
For I first beheld thy heart
On the night I last saw thee.
Pine-woods and mysteries!
Sea-sands and sorrows!
Hearts fluttered by a breeze
That bodes dark morrows, morrows,—
Bodes dark morrows!

Moonlight in sweet overflow
Poured upon the earth and sea!
Lovelight with intenser glow
In the deeps of thee and me!
Clasped hands and silences!
Hearts faint and throbbing!
The weak wind sighing in the trees!
The strong surf sobbing, sobbing,—
The strong surf sobbing!

A HILL SONG.

Hills where once my love and I
Let the hours go laughing by!
All your woods and dales are sad,—
You have lost your Oread.
Falling leaves! Silent woodlands!
Half your loveliness is fled.
Golden-rod, wither now!
Winter winds, come hither now!
All the summer joy is dead.

There's a sense of something gone
In the grass I linger on.
There's an under-voice that grieves
In the rustling of the leaves.
Pine-clad peaks! Rushing waters!
Glens where we were once so glad!
There's a light passed from you,
There's a joy outcast from you,—
You have lost your Oread.

AT SEA.

As a brave man faces the foe,
Alone against hundreds, and sees Death grin in his teeth,
But, shutting his lips, fights on to the end
Without speech, without hope, without flinching,—
So, silently, grimly, the steamer
Lurches ahead through the night.

A beacon-light far off,
Twinkling across the waves like a star!
But no star in the dark overhead!
The splash of waters at the prow, and the evil light
Of the death-fires flitting like will-o'-the-wisps beneath! And
beyond
Silence and night!

I sit by the taffrail,
Alone in the dark and the blown cold mist and the spray,
Feeling myself swept on irresistibly,
Sunk in the night and the sea, and made one with their footfall-
less onrush,
Letting myself be borne like a spar adrift
Helplessly into the night.

Without fear, without wish,
Insensate save of a dull, crushed ache in my heart,
Careless whither the steamer is going,
Conscious only as in a dream of the wet and the dark
And of a form that looms and fades indistinctly
Everywhere out of the night.

O love, how came I here?
Shall I wake at thy side and smile at my dream?
The dream that grips me so hard that I cannot wake nor stir!
O love! O my own love, found but to be lost!

My soul sends over the waters a wild inarticulate cry,
Like a gull's scream heard in the night.

The mist creeps closer. The beacon
Vanishes astern. The sea's monotonous noises
Lapse through the drizzle with a listless, subsiding cadence.
And thou, O love, and the sea throb on in my brain together,
While the steamer plunges along,
Butting its way through the night.

ISABEL.

In her body's perfect sweet
Suppleness and languor meet,—
Arms that move like lapsing billows,
Breasts that Love would make his pillows,
Eyes where vision melts in bliss,
Lips that ripen to a kiss.

CONTEMPORARIES.

"A barbered woman's man,"—yes, so
He seemed to me a twelvemonth since;
And so he may be—let it go—
Admit his flaws—we need not wince
To find our noblest not all great.
What of it? He is still the prince,
And we the pages of his state.

The world applauds his words; his fame
Is noised wherever knowledge be;
Even the trader hears his name,
As one far inland hears the sea;
The lady quotes him to the beau
Across a cup of Russian tea;
They know him and they do not know.

I know him. In the nascent years
Men's eyes shall see him as one crowned;
His voice shall gather in their ears
With each new age prophetic sound;
And you and I and all the rest,
Whose brows to-day are laurel-bound,
Shall be but plumes upon his crest.

A year ago this man was poor,—

This Alfred whom the nations praise;
He stood a beggar at my door
For one mere word to help him raise
From fainting limbs and shoulders bent
The burden of the weary days;
And I withheld it—and he went.

I knew him then, as I know now,
Our largest heart, our loftiest mind;
Yet for the curls upon his brow
And for his lisp, I could not find
The helping word, the cheering touch.
Ah, to be just, as well as kind,—
It costs so little and so much!

It seemed unmanly in my sight
That he, whose spirit was so strong
To lead the blind world to the light,
Should look so like the mincing throng
Who advertise the tailor's art.
It angered me—I did him wrong—
I grudged my groat and shut my heart.

I might have been the prophet's friend,
Helped him who is to help the world!
Now, when the striving is at end,
The reek-stained battle-banners furled,
And the age hears its muster-call,
Then I, because his hair was curled,
I shall have lost my chance—that's all.

THE TWO BOBBIES.

Bobbie Burns and Bobbie Browning,
They're the boys I'd like to see.
Though I'm not the boy for Bobbie,
Bobbie is the boy for me!

Bobbie Browning was the good boy;
Turned the language inside out,
Wrote his plays and had his days,
Died—and held his peace, no doubt.

Poor North Bobbie was the bad boy,—
Bad, bad, bad, bad Bobbie Burns!
Loved and made the world his lover,

Kissed and barleycomed by turns.

London's dweller, child of wisdom,
Kept his counsel, took his toll;
Ayrshire's vagrant paid the piper,
Lost the game—God save his soul!

Bobbie Burns and Bobbie Browning,
What's the difference, you see?
Bob the lover, Bob the lawyer;
Bobbie is the boy for me!

A TOAST.

Here's a health to thee, Roberts,
And here's a health to me;
And here's to all the pretty girls
From Denver to the sea!

Here's to mine and here's to thine!
Now's the time to clink it!
Here's a flagon of old wine,
And here are we to drink it.

Wine that maketh glad the heart
Of the bully boy!
Here's the toast that we love most,
"Love and song and joy!"

Song that is the flower of love,
And joy that is the fruit!
Here's the love of woman, lad,
And here's our love to boot!

You and I are far too wise
Not to fill our glasses.
Here's to me and here's to thee,
And here's to all the lasses!

THE KAVANAGH.

A stone jug and a pewter mug,
And a table set for three!
A jug and a mug at every place,
And a biscuit or two with Brie!
Three stone jugs of Cruiskeen Lawn,

And a cheese like crusted foam!
The Kavanagh receives to-night!
McMurrough is at home!

We three and the barley-bree!
And a health to the one away,
Who drifts down careless Italy,
God's wanderer and estray!
For friends are more than Arno's store
Of garnered charm, and he
Were blither with us here the night
Than Titian bids him be.

Throw ope the window to the stars,
And let the warm night in!
Who knows what revelry in Mars
May rhyme with rouse akin?
Fill up and drain the loving cup
And leave no drop to waste!
The moon looks in to see what's up—
Begad, she'd like a taste!

What odds if Leinster's kingly roll
Be now an idle thing?
The world is his who takes his toll,
A vagrant or a king.
What though the crown be melted down,
And the heir a gypsy roam?
The Kavanagh receives to-night!
McMurrough is at home!

We three and the barley-bree!
And the moonlight on the floor!
Who were a man to do with less?
What emperor has more?
Three stone jugs of Cruiskeen Lawn,
And three stout hearts to drain
A slanter to the truth in the heart of youth
And the joy of the love of men.

A CAPTAIN OF THE PRESS-GANG.

Shipmate, leave the ghostly shadows,
Where thy boon companions throng!
We will put to sea together
Through the twilight with a song.

Leering closer, rank and girding,
In this Black Port where we bide,
Reel a thousand flaring faces;
But escape is on the tide.

Let the tap-rooms of the city
Reek till the red dawn comes round.
There is better wine in plenty
On the cruise where we are bound.

I've aboard a hundred messmates
Better than these 'long-shore knaves.
There is wreckage on the shallows;
It's the open sea that saves.

Hark, lad, dost not hear it calling?
That's the voice thy father knew,
When he took the King's good cutlass
In his grip, and fought it through.

Who would palter at press-money
When he heard that sea-cry vast?
That's the call makes lords of lubbers,
When they ship before the mast.

Let thy cronies of the tavern
Keep their kisses bought with gold;
On the high seas there are regions
Where the heart is never old,

Where the great winds every morning
Sweep the sea-floor clean and white,
And upon the steel-blue arches
Burnish the great stars of night;

There the open hand will lose not,
Nor the loosened tongue betray.
Signed, and with our sailing orders,
We will clear before the day;

On the shining yards of heaven
See a wider dawn unfurled....
The eternal slaves of beauty
Are the masters of the world.

THE BUCCANEERS.

Oh, not for us the easy mirth
Of men that never roam!
The crackling of the narrow hearth,
The cabined joys of home!
Keep your tame, regulated glee,
O pale protected State!
Our dwelling-place is on the sea,
Our joy the joy of Fate!

No long caresses give us ease,
No lazy languors warm,
We seize our mates as the sea-gulls seize,
And leave them to the storm.
But in the bridal halls of gloom
The couch is stern and strait;
For us the marriage rite of Doom,
The nuptial joy of Fate.

Wine for the weaklings of the town,
Their lucky toasts to drain!
Our skoal for them whose star goes down,
Our drink the drink of men!
No Bacchic ivy for our brows!
Like vikings, we await
The grim, ungarlanded carouse
We keep to-night with Fate.

Ho, gamesters of the pampered court!
What stakes are those at strife?
Your thousands are but paltry sport
To them that play for life.
You risk doubloons, and hold your breath.
Win groats, and wax elate;
But we throw loaded dice with Death,
And call the turn on Fate.

The kings of earth are crowned with care,
Their poets wail and sigh;
Our music is to do and dare,
Our empire is to die.
Against the storm we fling our glee
And shout, till Time abate
The exultation of the sea,
The fearful joy of Fate.

THE WAR-SONG OF GAMELBAR.

Bowmen, shout for Gamelbar!
Winds, unthrottle the wolves of war!
Heave a breath
And dare a death
For the doom of Gamelbar!
Wealth for Gamel,
Wine for Gamel,
Crimson wine for Gamelbar!

CHORUS:—

Oh, sleep for a knave,

With his sins in the sod!

And death for the brave,

With his glory up to God!

And joy for the girl,

And ease for the churl!

But the great game of war

For our lord Gamelbar,

Gamelbar!
Spearmen, shout for Gamelbar,
With his Saxon thirty score!
Heave a sword
For our overlord,
Lord of warriors, Gamelbar!
Life for Gamel,
Love for Gamel,
Lady-loves for Gamelbar!

Horsemen, shout for Gamelbar!
Swim the ford and climb the scaur!
Heave a hand
For the maiden land,
The maiden land of Gamelbar!
Glory for Gamel,
Gold for Gamel,
Yellow gold for Gamelbar!

Armorers for Gamelbar,
Rivet and forge and fear no scar!
Heave a hammer

With anvil clamor,
To weld and brace for Gamelbar!
Ring for Gamel!
Rung for Gamel!
Ring-rung-ring for Gamelbar!

Yeomen, shout for Gamelbar,
And his battle-hand in war!
Heave his pennon;
Cheer his men on,
In the ranks of Gamelbar!
Strength for Gamel,
Song for Gamel,
One war-song for Gamelbar!

Roncliffe, shout for Gamelbar!
Menthorpe, Bryan, Castelfar!
Heave, Thorparch
Of the Waving Larch,
And Spofford's thane, for Gamelbar!
Blaise for Gamel,
Brame for Gamel,
Rougharlington for Gamelbar!

Maidens; strew for Gamelbar
Roses down his way to war!
Heave a handful,
Fill the land full
Of your gifts to Gamelbar!
Dream of Gamel,
Dance for Gamel,
Dance in the halls for Gamelbar!

Servitors, shout for Gamelbar!
Roast the ox and stick the boar!
Heave a bone
To gaunt Harone,
The great war-hound of Gamelbar!
Mead for Gamel,
Mirth for Gamel,
Mirth at the board for Gamelbar!

Trumpets, speak for Gamelbar!
Blare as ye never blared before!
Heave a bray

In the horns to-day,
The red war-horns of Gamelbar!
To-night for Gamel,
The North for Gamel,
With fires on the hills for Gamelbar!

Shout for Gamel, Gamelbar,
Till your throats can shout no more!
Heave a cry
As he rideth by,
Sons of Orm, for Gamelbar!
Folk for Gamel,
Fame for Gamel,
Years and fame for Gamelbar!

CHORUS:—

Oh, sleep for a knave

With his sins in the sod!

And death for the brave,

With his glory up to God!

And joy for the girl,

And ease for the churl!

But the great game of war

For our lord Gamelbar,

Gamelbar!

THE OUTLAW.

Oh, let my lord laugh in his halls
When he the tale shall tell!
But woe to Jarlwell and its walls
When I shall laugh as well!
And he that laughs the last, lads,
Laughs well, laughs well!

He's lord of many a burg and farm
And mickle thralls and gold,
And I am but my own right arm,
My dwelling-place the wold.
But when we twain meet face to face,
He will hot laugh so bold.

The shame he chuckles as he shows
This time he need not tell;
I'll give his body to the crows,
And his black soul to Hell.
For he that laughs the last, lads,
Laughs well, laughs well!

THE KING'S SON.

"Daughter, daughter, marry no man,
Though a king's son come to woo,
If he be not more than blessing or ban
To the secret soul of you."

"'Tis the King's son, indeed, I ween,
And he left me even but now,
And he shall make me a dazzling queen,
With a gold crown on my brow."

"And are you one that a golden crown,
Or the lust of a name can lure?
You had better wed with a country clown,
And keep your young heart pure."

"Mother, the King has sworn, and said
That his son shall wed but me;
And I must gang to the prince's bed,
Or a traitor I shall be."

"Oh, what care you for an old man's wrath?
Or what care you for a king?
I had rather you fled on an outlaw's path,
A rebel, a hunted thing."

"Mother, it is my father's will,
For the King has promised him fair
A goodly earldom of hollow and hill,
And a coronet to wear."

"Then woe is worth a father's name,
For it names your dourest foe!
I had rather you came the child of shame
Than to have you fathered so."

"Mother, I shall have gold enow,

Though love be never mine,
To buy all else that the world can show
Of good and fair and fine."

"Oh, what care you for a prince's gold,
Or the key of a kingdom's till?
I had rather see you a harlot bold
That sins of her own free will.

"For I have been wife for the stomach's sake,
And I know whereof I say;
A harlot is sold for a passing slake,
But a wife is sold for aye.

"Body and soul for a lifetime sell,
And the price of the sale shall be
That you shall be harlot and slave as well
Until Death set you free."

LAURANA'S SONG. FOR "A LADY OF VENICE."

Who'll have the crumpled pieces of a heart?
Let him take mine!
Who'll give his whole of passion for a part,
And call't divine?
Who'll have the soiled remainder of desire?
Who'll warm his fingers at a burnt-out fire?
Who'll drink the lees of love, and cast i' the mire
The nobler wine?

Let him come here, and kiss me on the mouth,
And have his will!
Love dead and dry as summer in the South
When winds are still
And all the leafage shrivels in the heat!
Let him come here and linger at my feet
Till he grow weary with the over-sweet,
And die, or kill.

LAUNA DEE.

Weary, oh, so weary
With it all!
Sunny days or dreary—
How they pall!
Why should we be heroes,

Launa Dee,
Striving to no winning?
Let the world be Zero's!
As in the beginning
Let it be!

What good comes of toiling,
When all's done?
Frail green sprays for spoiling
Of the sun;
Laurel leaf or myrtle,
Love or fame—
Ah, what odds what spray, sweet?
Time, that makes life fertile,
Makes its blooms decay, sweet,
As they came.

Lie here with me dreaming,
Cheek to cheek,
Lithe limbs twined and gleaming,
Brown and sleek;
Like two serpents coiling
In their lair.
Where's the good of wreathing
Sprays for Time's despoiling?
Let me feel your breathing
In my hair.

You and I together—
Was it so?
In the August weather
Long ago!
Did we kiss and fellow,
Side by side,
Till the sunbeams quickened
From our stalks great yellow
Sunflowers, till we sickened
There and died?

Were we tigers creeping
Through the glade
Where our prey lay sleeping,
Unafraid,
In some Eastern jungle?
Better so.

I am sure the snarling
Beasts could never bungle
Life as men do, darling,
Who half know.

Ah, if all of life, love,
Were the living!
Just to cease from strife, love,
And from grieving;
Let the swift world pass us,
You and me,
Stilled from all aspiring,—
Sinai nor Parnassus
Longer worth desiring,
Launa Dee!

Just to live like lilies
In the lake!
Where no thought nor will is,
To mistake!
Just to lose the human
Eyes that weep!
Just to cease from seeming
Longer man and woman!
Just to reach the dreaming
And the sleep!

THE MENDICANTS.

We are as mendicants who wait
Along the roadside in the sun.
Tatters of yesterday and shreds
Of morrow clothe us every one.

And some are dotards, who believe
And glory in the days of old;
While some are dreamers, harping still
Upon an unknown age of gold.

Hopeless or witless! Not one heeds,
As lavish Time comes down the way
And tosses in the suppliant hat
One great new-minted gold To-day.

Ungrateful heart and grudging thanks,
His beggar's wisdom only sees

Housing and bread and beer enough;
He knows no other things than these.

O foolish ones, put by your care!
Where wants are many, joys are few;
And at the wilding springs of peace,
God keeps an open house for you.

But that some Fortunatus' gift
Is lying there within his hand,
More costly than a pot of pearls,
His dulness does not understand.

And so his creature heart is filled;
His shrunken self goes starved away.
Let him wear brand-new garments still,
Who has a threadbare soul, I say.

But there be others, happier few,
The vagabondish sons of God,
Who know the by-ways and the flowers,
And care not how the world may plod.

They idle down the traffic lands,
And loiter through the woods with spring;
To them the glory of the earth
Is but to hear a bluebird sing.

They too receive each one his Day;
But their wise heart knows many things
Beyond the sating of desire,
Above the dignity of kings.

One I remember kept his coin,
And laughing flipped it in the air;
But when two strolling pipe-players
Came by, he tossed it to the pair.

Spendthrift of joy, his childish heart
Danced to their wild outlandish bars;
Then supperless he laid him down
That night, and slept beneath the stars.

THE MARCHING MORROWS.

Now gird thee well for courage,
My knight of twenty year,
Against the marching morrows
That fill the world with fear!

The flowers fade before them;
The summer leaves the hill;
Their trumpets range the morning,
And those who hear grow still.

Like pillagers of harvest,
Their fame is far abroad,
As gray remorseless troopers
That plunder and maraud.

The dust is on their corselets;
Their marching fills the world;
With conquest after conquest
Their banners are unfurled.

They overthrow the battles
Of every lord of war,
From world-dominioned cities
Wipe out the names they bore.

Sohrab, Rameses, Roland,
Ramoth, Napoleon, Tyre,
And the Romeward Huns of Attila—
Alas, for their desire!

By April and by autumn
They perish in their pride,
And still they close and gather
Out of the mountain-side.

The tanned and tameless children
Of the wild elder earth,
With stature of the northlights,
They have the stars for girth.

There's not a hand to stay them,
Of all the hearts that brave;
No captain to undo them,
No cunning to off-stave.

Yet fear thou not! If haply
Thou be the kingly one,
They'll set thee in their vanguard
To lead them round the sun.

IN THE WORKSHOP.

Once in the Workshop, ages ago,
The clay was wet and the fire was low.

And He who was bent on fashioning man
Moulded a shape from a clod,
And put the loyal heart therein;
While another stood watching by.

"What's that?" said Beelzebub.
"A lover," said God.
And Beelzebub frowned, for he knew that kind.

And then God fashioned a fellow shape
As lithe as a willow rod,
And gave it the merry roving eye
And the range of the open road.

"What's that?" said Beelzebub.
"A vagrant," said God.
And Beelzebub smiled, for he knew that kind.

And last of all God fashioned a form,
And gave it, what was odd,
The loyal heart and the roving eye;
And he whistled, light of care.

"What's that?" said Beelzebub.
"A poet," said God.
And Beelzebub frowned, for he did not know.

THE MOTE.

Two shapes of august bearing, seraph tall,
Of indolent imperturbable regard,
Stood in the Tavern door to drink. As the first
Lifted his glass to let the warm light melt
In the slow bubbles of the wine, a sunbeam,
Red and broad as smouldering autumn, smote
Down through its mystery; and a single fleck,

The tiniest sun-mote settling through the air,
Fell on the grape-dark surface and there swam.

Gently the Drinker with fastidious care
Stretched hand to clear the speck away. "No, no!"—
His comrade stayed his arm. "Why," said the first,
"What would you have me do?" "Ah, let it float
A moment longer!" And the second smiled.
"Do you not know what that is?" "No, indeed."
"A mere dust-mote, a speck of soot, you think,
A plague-germ still unsatisfied. It is not.
That is the Earth. See, I will stretch my hand
Between it and the sun; the passing shadow
Gives its poor dwellers a glacial period.
Let it but stand an hour, it would dissolve,
Intangible as the color of the wine.
There, throw it away now! Lift it from the sweet
Enveloping flood it has enjoyed so well;"
(He smiled as only those who live can smile)
"Its time is done, its revelry complete,
Its being accomplished. Let us drink again."

IN THE HOUSE OF IDIEDAILY.

Oh, but life went gayly, gayly,
In the house of Idiedaily!

There were always throats to sing
Down the river-banks with spring,

When the stir of heart's desire
Set the sapling's heart on fire.

Bobolincolns in the meadows,
Leisure in the purple shadows,

Till the poppies without number
Bowed their heads in crimson slumber,

And the twilight came to cover
Every unreluctant lover.

Not a night but some brown maiden
Bettered all the dusk she strayed in,

While the roses in her hair

Bankrupted oblivion there.

Oh, but life went gayly, gayly,
In the house of Idiedaily!

But this hostelry, The Barrow,
With its chambers, bare and narrow,

Mean, ill-windowed, damp, and wormy,
Where the silence makes you squirmy,

And the guests are never seen to,
Is a vile place, a mere lean-to,

Not a traveller speaks well of,
Even worse than I heard tell of,

Mouldy, ramshackle, and foul.
What a dwelling for a soul!

Oh, but life went gayly, gayly,
In the house of Idiedaily!

There the hearth was always warm,
From the slander of the storm.

There your comrade was your neighbor,
Living on to-morrow's labor.

And the board was always steaming,
Though Sir Ringlets might be dreaming.

Not a plate but scoffed at porridge,
Not a cup but floated borage.

There were always jugs of sherry
Waiting for the makers merry,

And the dark Burgundian wine
That would make a fool divine.

Oh, but life went gayly, gayly
In the house of Idiedaily!

RESIGNATION.

When I am only fit to go to bed,
Or hobble out to sit within the sun,
Ring down the curtain, say the play is done,
And the last petals of the poppy shed!

I do not want to live when I am old,
I have no use for things I cannot love;
And when the day that I am talking of
(Which God forfend!) is come, it will be cold.

But if there is another place than this,
Where all the men will greet me as "Old Man,"
And all the women wrap me in a smile,
Where money is more useless than a kiss,
And good wine is not put beneath the ban,
I will go there and stay a little while.

COMRADES.

Comrades, pour the wine to-night
For the parting is with dawn!
Oh, the clink of cups together,
With the daylight coming on!
Greet the morn
With a double horn,
When strong men drink together!

Comrades, gird your swords to-night,
For the battle is with dawn!
Oh, the clash of shields together,
With the triumph coming on!
Greet the foe,
And lay him low,
When strong men fight together!

Comrades, watch the tides to-night,
For the sailing is with dawn!
Oh, to face the spray together,
With the tempest coming on!
Greet the sea
With a shout of glee,
When strong men roam together!

Comrades, give a cheer to-night,
For the dying is with dawn!
Oh, to meet the stars together,

With the silence coming on!
Greet the end
As a friend a friend,
When strong men die together!

THE END

MORE SONGS FROM VAGABONDIA

Bliss Carman Richard Hovey

1896,

BY BLISS CARMAN AND RICHARD HOVEY.

To M. G. M., so good to lighten cares,
The boys inscribe this second book of theirs.

And ever with the vanguard

The vagrant singers come

The gamins of the city

Who dance before the drum

A VAGABOND SONG.

There is something in the autumn that is native to my blood--
Touch of manner, hint of mood;
And my heart is like a rhyme,
With the yellow and the purple and the crimson keeping time.
The scarlet of the maples can shake me like a cry
Of bugles going by.
And my lonely spirit thrills
To see the frosty asters like a smoke upon the hills.
There is something in October sets the gypsy blood astir;
We must rise and follow her,
When from every hill of flame
She calls and calls each vagabond by name.

JONGLEURS.

What is the stir in the street?
Hurry of feet!
And after,
A sound as of pipes and of tabers!

Men of the conflicts and labors,
Struggling and shifting and shoving,
Pushing and pounding your neighbors,
Fighting for leeway for laughter,
Toiling for leisure for loving!
Hark, through the window and up to the rafter,
Madder and merrier,
Deeper and verier,
Sweeter, contrarier,
Dafter and dafter,
A song arises,--
A thrill, an intrusion,
A reel, an illusion,
A rapture, a crisis
Of bells in the air!

Ay, up from your work and look out of the window!
"Who are the newcomers, Arab or Hindoo?
Persians, or Japs, or the children of Isis?"
--Guesses, surmises--
Forth with you, fare
Down in the street to draw nearer and stare!
Come from your palaces, come from your hovels!

Lay down your ledgers, your picks and your shovels,
Your trowels and bricks,
Hammers and nails,
Scythes and flails,
Bargains and sales,
And the trader's tricks,
Deals, overreachings,
Worries and griefs,
Teachings and preachings,
Boluses, briefs,
Writs and attachments,
Quarterings, hatchments,
Clans and cognomens,
Comments and scholia,
(World's melancholia)--
Cast them aside, and good riddance to rubbish!
Here at the street-corner, hearken, a strain,
Rough and off-hand and a bit rub-a-dub-ish,
Gives us a taste of the life we'd attain.

Who are they, what are they, whence have they come to us?
Where will they go.when their singing is done?
What is the garb they wear, tattered and sumptuous,
Faded with days and superb in the sun?
What are they singing of?
Hush!
... There's a ringing of
Delicate chimes;
And the blush
Of a veiled bride morning
Beats in the rhymes.
Listen!
Out of the merriment,
Clear as the glisten
Of dew on the brier,
A silver warning!
Sudden, a dare--
Lyric experiment--
Up like a lark in the air,
Higher and higher and higher,
The song shoots out of our blunder
Of thought to the blue sky of wonder,
And broken strains only fall down
Like pearls on the roofs of the town.

Somebody says they have come from the moon,
Seen with their eyes Eldorado,
Sat in the Bo-tree's shadow,
Wandered at noon
In the valleys of Van,
Tented in Lebanon, tarried in Ophir,
Last year in Tartary piped for the Khan.
Now it's the song of a lover;
Now it's the lilt of a loafer,--
Under the trees in a midsummer noon,
Dreaming the haze into isles to discover,
Beating the silences into a croon;
Soon
Up from the marshes a fall of the plover!
Out from the cover
A flurry of quail!
Down from the height where the slow hawks hover,
The thin far ghost of a hail!
And near, and near,
Throbbing and tingling,--
With a human cheer
In the earth-song mingling,--
Mirth and carousal,
Wooing, espousal,
Clinking of glasses
And laughter of lasses--
And the wind in the garden stoops down as it passes
To play with the hair
Of the loveliest there,
And the wander-lust catches the will in its snare;
Hill-wind and spray-lure,
Call of the heath;
Dare in the teeth
Of the balk and the failure;
The clasp and the linger
Of loosening finger,
Loth to dissever;
Thrill of the comrade heart to its fellow
Through droughts that sicken and blasts that bellow
From purple furrow to harvest yellow,
Now and forever.
How our feet itch to keep time to their measure!
How our hearts lift to the lilt of their song!
Let the world go, for a day's royal pleasure!
Not every summer such waifs come along.

Now they are off to the inn;
Hear the clean ring of their laughter!
Cool as a hill-brook after
The beat of the noon sets in!
Gentlemen even in jollity--
Certainly people of quality!--
Waifs and estrays no less,
Roofless and penniless,
They are the wayside strummers
Whose lips are man's renown,
Those wayward brats of Summer's
Who stroll from town to town;
Spendthrift of life, they ravish
The days of an endless store,
And ever the more they lavish
The heap of the hoard is more.
For joy and love and vision
Are alive and breed and stay
When dust shall hold in derision
The misers of a day.

EARTH'S LYRIC.

April. You hearken, my fellow,
Old slumberer down in my heart?
There's a whooping of ice in the rivers;
The sap feels a start.

The snow-melted torrents are brawling;
The hills, orange-misted and blue,
Are touched with the voice of the rainbird
Unsullied and new.

The houses of frost are deserted,
Their slumber is broken and done,
And empty and pale are the portals
Awaiting the sun.

The bands of Arcturus are slackened;
Orion goes forth from his place
On the slopes of the night, leading homeward
His hound from the chase.

The Pleiades weary and follow
The dance of the ghostly dawn;
The revel of silence is over;
Earth's lyric comes on.

A golden flute in the cedars,
A silver pipe in the swales,
And the slow large life of the forest
Wells bade and prevails.

A breath of the woodland spirit
Has blown out the bubble of spring
To this tenuous hyaline glory
One touch sets a-wing.

THE WOOD-GOD.

Brother, lost brother!
Thou of mine ancient kin!
Thou of the swift will that no ponderings smother!
The dumb life in me fumbles out to the shade
Thou lurkest in.
In vain--evasive ever through the glade
Departing footsteps fail;
And only where the grasses have been pressed,
Or by snapped twigs I follow a fruitless trail.
So--give o'er the quest!
Sprawl on the roots and moss!
Let the lithe garter squirm across my throat!
Let the slow clouds and leaves above me float
Into mine eyeballs and across,--
Nor think them further! Lo, the marvel! now,
Thou whom my soul desireth, even thou
Sprawl'st by my side, who fled'st at my pursuit.
I hear thy fluting; at my shoulder there
I see the sharp ears through the tangled hair,
And birds and bunnies at thy music mute.

A FAUN'S SONG.

Cool! cool! cool!
Cool and sweet
The feel of the moss at my feet!

And sweet and cool
The touch of the wind, of the wind!

Cool wind out of the blue,
At the touch of you
A little wave crinkles and flows
All over me down to my toes.

"Coo-loo! Coo-loo!"
Hear the doves in the tree-tops croon.
"Coo-loo! Coo-loo!"
Love comes soon.

"June! June!"
The veery sings,
Sings and sings,
"June! June!"--
A pretty tune!

Wind with your weight of perfume,
Bring me the bluebells' bloom!

QUINCE TO LILAC:TO G. H.

Dear *Lilac*, how enchanting
To hear of you this way!
The Man who comes a-mouching
To visit me each day

Says you too have a lover
Far lovelier than I.
And from his rapt description,
She loves you gloriously.

The Man prowls out each morning
To see if spring's begun.
What infinite amusement
These creatures offer one!

He asks me such conundrums
As no one ever heard:
The name of April's father,
The trail of every bird,

What keeps me warm in winter,
Who wakes me up in time,
And why procrastination
Is such a fearful crime.

And yet, who knows? He may be
Our equal ages hence--
With such pathetic glimmers
Of weird intelligence!

But this your blessed alien,
Why strays she roving here?
Was Orpheus not her brother,
Persephone her peer?

Was she not once a dryad
Whom Syrinx lulled to sleep
Beside the Dorian water,
And still her eyelids keep

The glad unperished secret
From centuries of joy,
And memories of the morning
When Helen sailed for Troy?

Is her name Gertrude, Kitty,
Hypatia, or what?
I seem to half remember,
And yet have quite forgot.

That soft Hellenic laughter!
I marvel you don't make
An effort to be early
In budding for her sake.

Just fancy hearing daily
That velvet voice of hers!
How do you quell the riot
Of sap her coming stirs?

Perhaps she puts her face up,
(Dear Charity she is!)

For messages of summer
And better worlds than this.

You cannot blush, poor Lilac;
It is not in your race.
I simply should go crimson,
If I were in your place.

Do tell her all your secrets!
The Man declares she knows
Better than any mortal
The wonder-trick of prose.

Our prose, I mean,--how beauty
Appears to you and me;
The truth that seems so simple,
Which they call poetry.

They put it down in writing
And label it with tags,
The funny conscious people
Who mask in colored rags!

They have a thing called *science*,
With phrases strange and pat.
My dear, can you imagine
Intelligence like that?

And when they first discover
That yellows are not greens,
They pucker up their foreheads
And ponder what it means.

And then those cave-like places,
Churches and Capitols,
Where they all come together
Like troops of talking dolls,

To govern, as they term it,
(It's really very odd!)
And have what they call worship
Of something they call God.

But Kitty, or whatever
May be her tender name,
Is more like us. She guesses
What sets the year aflame.

She knows beyond her senses;
Do tell her all you can!
The funny people need it,--
At least, so says The Man.

Good-by, dear. I must idle.
Sweet suns and happy rains!
How nice to have these humans
With their inventive brains,--

Their little scraps of paper!
They certainly evince
Remarkable discernment.
Your ever loving *Quince*.

AN EASTER MARKET.

Today, through your Easter market
In the lazy Southern sun,
I strolled with hands in pockets
Past the flower-stalls one by one.

Indolent, dreamy, ready
For anything to amuse,
Shyfoot out for a ramble
In his oldest hat and shoes.

Roses creamy and yellow,
Azaleas crimson and white,
And the flaky fresh carnations
My Orient of delight,--

Masses and banks of blossom
That dazzle and summon the eye,
Till the buyers are half bewildered
To know what they want. Not I.

Who would not rather be artist
And slip through the crowd unseen
To gather it all in a picture
And guess what the faces mean?

So down through the chaffering darkies
I pass to the sidewalk's end,
Through the smiling gingham bonnets
With their small farm-stuff to vend.

When, hello! my dreamer, sudden
As call at the dead of night,
What sets your pulses a-quiver,
What sets your fancy alight?

Sure of it! Mayflowers, mayflowers,
Scent of the North in spring!
Out in the vernal distance,
Heart of me, whither a-wing?

"Give me some!" Clutch the first handful,
Hungering rover of earth!
How I devour and kiss them,
Beauties that brought me to birth,

Away in the great north country,
The land of the lonely sun,
Where God has few for his fellows,
And the wolves of the snowdrift run.

Once more to the frost-bound valley
Comes April with rain in her jar;
I can hear the vesper sparrow
Under the silver star.

And many and dear and gracious
Are the dreams that walk at my side
From the land of the lingering shadows,
As out of the throng I stride.

Oh, well for you, mere onlooker,
Who drift through the world's great mart!

But we of the human sorrow
Have a joy beyond your art.

DAISIES.

Over the shoulders and slopes of the dune
I saw the white daisies go down to the sea,
A host in the sunshine, an army in June,
The people God sends us to set our heart free.

The bobolinks rallied them up from the dell,
The orioles whistled them out of the wood;
And all of their singing was, "Earth, it is well!"
And all of their dancing was, "Life, thou art good!"

THE MOCKING-BIRD.

Hear! hear! hear!
Listen! the word
Of the mocking-bird!
Hear! hear! hear!
I will make all clear;
I will let you know
Where the footfalls go
That through the thicket and over the hill
Allure, allure.
How the bird-voice cleaves
Through the weft of leaves
With a leap and a thrill
Like the flash of a weaver's shuttle, swift and sudden and sure!

And la, he is gone--even while I turn
The wisdom of his runes to learn.
He knows the mystery of the wood,
The secret of the solitude;
But he will not tell, he will not tell,
For all he promises so well.

KARLENE.

Word of a little one born in the West,--
How like a sea-bird it comes from the sea,

Out of the league-weary waters' unrest
Blown with white wings, for a token, to me!

Blown with a skriel and a flurry of plumes
(Sea-spray and flight-rapture whirled in a gleam!)
Here for a sign of the comrade that looms
Large in the mist of my love as I dream.

He with the heart of an old violin,
Vibrant at every least stir in the place,
Lyric of woods where the thrushes begin,
Wave-questing wanderer, still for a space,--

What will the child of his be (so I muse),
Wood-flower, sea-flower, star-flower rare?
Worlds here to choose from, and which will she choose,
She whose first world is an armsweep of air?

Baby Karlene, you are wondering now
Why you can't reach the great moon that you see
Just at your hand on the edge of the bough
That waves in the window-pane--how can it be?

All your world yet hardly lies out of reach
Of ten little fingers and ten little toes.
You are a seed for the sky there to teach
(And the sun and the wind and the rain) as it grows.

Just a green leaf piercing up to the day,
Pale fleck of June to come, just to be seen
Through the rough crumble of rubble and clay
Lifting its loveliness, dawn-child, Karlene!

Fragile as fairycraft, dew-dream of love,--
Never a clod that has marred the slim stalk,
Never a stone but its frail fingers move,
Bent on the blue sky and nothing can balk!

Blue sky and wind-laughters, that is thy dream.
Ah the brave days when thy leafage shall toss
High where gold noondays and sunsets a-stream
Mix with its moving and kiss it across.

There the great clouds shall go lazily by,
Coo! thee with shadows and dazzle with shine,
Drench thee with rain-guerdons, bless thee with sky,
Till all the knowledge of earth shall be thine.

Wind from the ice-floe and wind from the palm,
Wind from the mountains and wind from the lea--
How they will sing thee of tempest and calm!
How they will lure thee with tales of the sea!

What will you be in that summer, Karlene?
Apple-tree, cherry-tree, lily, or corn?
Red rose or yellow rose, gray leaf or green?
Which will you choose now the year's at its morn?

Somewhere even now in thy heart is the will,--
"I shall be Golden Rod, slender and tall--
I shall be Pond Lily, secret and still--
I shall be Sweetbriar, Queen of them all--

"I shall give shade for the weary to rest--
I shall grow flax for the naked to wear--
Figs for a feast and all comers to guest--
Wreaths that girls twine in the laugh of their hair--

"Ivy for scholars and myrtle for lovers,
Laurel for conquerors, poets, and kings--
Broad-spreading beech-boughs whose benison covers
Clamor of bird-notes and flutter of wings--

"I shall rise tall as an elm in my grace--
I shall be clothed as catalpa is clad--
Poets shall crown me with lyrics of praise--
Lovers for lure of my blossoms go mad!"

Which shall it be, baby? Guess you at all?
Only I know in the lull of the year
You have said now where your choosing shall fall,
Only you have not yet heard yourself, dear.

So, like a mocking-bird, up in the trees,
I watching wondering where you have grown,

Borrow a note from a birdfellow's glees,
Fittest to sing you, and make it my own.

Only I know as I wonder, Karlene,
Singing up here where you think me a star,
Heaven's still above me, and some one serene
Laughs in the blue sky and knows what you are.

KARLENE.

Good-morning, Karlene. It's a very
Fine beautiful world we are in.
Well, you *do* look as ripe as a berry;
And, pardon me, such a real chin!

And may I--Ah, thank you; the pleasure
Is mine; just one kiss by your ear!--
May I introduce myself as your
Most dutiful godfather, dear?

I have fumed, like champagne that is fizzy,
To pay my respects at your door.
But the publishers keep one *so* busy.
Forgive my not calling before!

Karlene, you're a very small lady
To venture so far all alone;
Especially into so shady
A place as this planet has grown.

When *I* now, my dear, was at *your* age,
When nobody tried to be rich,
But lived on high thinking and porridge
(And didn't know t' other from which!),

For a girl to go out unattended
Was considered "not only unwise
And improper--" Our grandmothers ended
By lifting to heaven their eyes.

And yet even now, though it's shocking
To slander these wonderful years,

I dare say an inch of black stocking
Could set all the world by the ears.

Black, mind you, not blue! It's a trifle;
But trifling in stockings won't do;
For love has an eye like a rifle
(His bandage is slipping askew).

But there! You are simply *too* charming.
No doubt you'll be modern enough
(Though the speed of the world is alarming)
To win with a delicate bluff,

As we say when we're raking the chips in,
On a hand that was not over strong--
But I see you are pursing your lips in;
Perhaps I am prating too long.

Anyhow you'll be learned in isms,
And talk pterodactyls in French,
And know polyhedrons from prisms,--
Though you may not know how to retrench.

You will fall out of love with digamma
To fall in again with Delsarte;
You will make a new Syriac grammar,
And know all the popes off by heart.

What Socrates said to Xantippe
When the lash of her tongue made him grieve;
What makes the banana peel slippy;
And what the snake whispered to Eve;

The music that Nero had played him,
When Rome was touched off with a match;
Why the king let the lady upbraid him
For burning her buns in a batch;

Why Hebrew is written left-handed;
And what Venus did with her arms;
What the Conqueror said when he landed;
The acres in Horace's farms;

The use of *hirundo* and *passer*.
All this you will probe to the pith
As a freshman at Wellesley or Vassar
Or Bryn Mawr--though *I* prefer Smith.

You will solve every riddle in Browning;
And learn how to paddle and swim;
And save other people from drowning;
And play basket ball in the gym.

But you'll scorn to know why there's a tax on
All reading that isn't a bore,
When Mallarmé's filtered through Saxon
And the Symbolists come to the fore.

All winter you'll read mathematics
(Oh, you'll be a terrible "prod"),
And in June, at the Senior Dramatics,
You will play like a star. But it's odd,

Since you'll quote every cadence in Kipling
And Arnold (of course I mean Matt),
If you don't make a bard of some stripling
Before he knows where he is at.

I am sure you'll be lovely as Trilby,
The loveliest bud of the year;
But remember, Karlene, I shall still be
Your doting old godfather, dear.

When you hear Archimedes' conundrum,
Like enough you'll be wanting to try
Whether one little girl *contra mundum*
Can't lift the old thing with a pry!

You will turn up your nose at poor "Thy will,"
With a haughty agnostical sniff,
Till you find the imperative "I will"
Has a future conditional "if."

And then you will come to your senses,
And find out why women were made;

And men too; and why there are fences
All round the whole lot where you strayed,

While you wore yourself down to a shadow
Yet failed to discover your sphere;
For you'll see Adam down in the meadow
And think what a goosey you were!

And then when your classmates are singing
Once more for good-by the old glees,
And the round painted lanterns are swinging
And sputtering out in the trees,

When everything stales and withers
Except the great stars up above,
Your heartstrings will all go to smithers,
You'll just be one crumple of love.

And Adam will be such a duffer
(Dear fellow, I mean), he'll contrive,
Till you make him, to not make him suffer,
The happiest mortal alive.

Oh, it makes me too ill to continue,
Imagining how it will be
When some dapper youth comes to win you
And smiles condescension on me!

I shall loathe his immaculate breeding,
And advise you in time to refuse.
To think he will share in your reading,
And even unbutton your shoes!

And yet when for that precious laddie
Your hair is all crinkled and curled,
I guess you'll be just like your daddy,
The dearest old soul in the world!

CONCERNING KAVIN.

When Kavin comes back from the barber,
Although he no longer is young,

One cheek is as soft as his heart,
And the other as smooth as his tongue. '

KAVIN AGAIN.

It is not anything he says,
It's just his presence and his smile,
The blarney of his silences
That cocker and beguile.

ACROSS THE TABLE.TO A. L. L.

Here's to you, Arthur! You and I
Have seen a lot of stormy weather,
Since first we clinked cups on the sly
At school together.

The winds of fate have had their will
And blown our crafts so far apart
We hardly knew if either still
Were on the chart.

But now I know the love of man
Is more than time or space or fate,
And laugh to scorn the powers that ban,
With you for mate.

It's good to have you sitting by,
Old man, to prove the world no botch,
To shame the devil with your eye
And pass the Scotch.

BARNEY MCGEE.

Barney McGee, there's no end of good luck in you,
Will-o'-the-wisp, with a flicker of Puck in you,
Wild as a bull-pup and all of his pluck in you,--
Let a man tread on your coat and he'll see!--
Eyes like the lakes of Killarney for clarity,
Nose that turns up without any vulgarity,
Smile like a cherub, and hair that is carroty,--
Wow, you're a rarity, Barney McGee!
Mellow as Tarragon,

Prouder than Aragon--
Hardly a paragon,
You will agree--
Here's all that's fine to you!
Books and old wine to you!
Girls be divine to you,
Barney McGee!

Lucky the day when I met you unwittingly,
Dining where vagabonds came and went flittingly.
Here's some *Barbera* to drink it befittingly,
That day at *Silvio's*, Barney McGee!
Many's the time we have quaffed our Chianti there,
Listened to Silvio quoting us Dante there,--
Once more to drink *Nebiolo spumante* there,
How we'd pitch Pommery into the sea!
There where the gang of us
Met ere Rome rang of us,
They had the hang of us
To a degree.
How they would trust to you!
That was but just to you.
Here's o'er their dust to you,
Barney McGee!

Barney McGee, when you're sober you scintillate,
But when you're in drink you're the pride of the intellect;
Divil a one of us ever came in till late,
Once at the bar where you happened to be--
Every eye there like a spoke in you centering,
You with your eloquence, blarney, and bantering--
All Vagabondia shouts at your entering,
King of the Tenderloin, Barney McGee!
There's no satiety
In your society
With the variety
Of your *esprit*.
Here's a long purse to you,
And a great thirst to you!
Fate be no worse to you,
Barney McGee!

Och, and the girls whose poor hearts you deracinate,
Whirl and bewilder and flutter and fascinate!
Faith, it's so killing you are, you assassinate,--

Murder's the word for you, Barney McGee!
Bold when they're sunny and smooth when they're showery,--
Oh, but the style of you, fluent and flowery!
Chesterfield's way, with a touch of the Bowery!
How would they silence you, Barney *machree?*
Naught can your gab allay,
Learned as Rabelais
(You in his abbey lay
Once on the spree).
Here's to the smile of you,
(Oh, but the guile of you!)
And a long while of you,
Barney McGee!

Facile with phrases of length and Latinity,
Like *honorificabilitudinity*,
Where is the maid could resist your vicinity,
Wiled by the impudent grace of your plea?
Then your vivacity and pertinacity
Carry the day with the divil's audacity;
No mere veracity robs your sagacity
Of perspicacity, Barney McGee.
When all is new to them,
What will you do to them?
Will you be true to them?
Who shall decree?
Here's a fair strife to you!
Health and long life to you!
And a great wife to you,
Barney McGee!

Barney McGee, you're the pick of gentility;
Nothing can phase you, you've such a facility;
Nobody ever yet found your utility,--
That is the charm of you, Barney McGee;
Under conditions that others would stammer in,
Still unperturbed as a cat or a Cameron,
Polished as somebody in the Decameron,
Putting the glamour on prince or Pawnee!
In your meanderin',
Love, and philanderin',
Calm as a mandarin
Sipping his tea!
Under the art of you,
Parcel and part of you,

Here's to the heart of you,
Barney McGee!

You who were ever alert to befriend a man,
You who were ever the first to defend a man,
You who had always the money to lend a man,
Down on his luck and hard up for a V!
Sure, you'll be playing a harp in beatitude
(And a quare sight you will be in that attitude)--
Some day, where gratitude seems but a platitude,
You'll find your latitude, Barney McGee.
That's no flim-flam at all,
Frivol or sham at all,
Just the plain--Damn it all,
Have one with me!
Here's luck and more to you!
Friends by the score to you,
True to the core to you,
Barney McGee!

THE SEA GYPSY.

I am fevered with the sunset,
I am fretful with the bay,
For the wander-thirst is on me
And my soul is in Cathay.

There's a schooner in the offing,
With her topsails shot with fire,
And my heart has gone aboard her
For the Islands of Desire.

I must forth again to-morrow!
With the sunset I must be
Hull down on the trail of rapture
In the wonder of the sea.

SPEECH AND SILENCE.

The words that pass from lip to lip
For souls still out of reach!
A friend for that companionship
That's deeper than all speech!

SECRETS.

Three secrets that never were said:
The stir of the sap in the spring,
The desire of a man to a maid,
The urge of a poet to sing.

THE FIRST JULEP.

I love the lazy Southern spring,
The way she melts around a chap
And lets the great magnolias fling
Their languid petals in his lap.

I love to travel down half-way
And meet her coming up the earth,
With hurdy-gurdy men who play
And make the children dance for mirth.

But best of all I love to steer
For quiet corners not too far,
Where the first juleps reappear
With fresh green mint behind the bar.

P. S. Perhaps you'll think it queer,
But I do not dislike a hint
To let the juleps disappear
And stick my nose into the mint.

A STEIN SONG.

Give a rouse, then, in the Maytime
For a life that knows no fear!
Turn night-time into daytime
With the sunlight of good cheer!
For it's always fair weather
When good fellows get together,
With a stein on the table and a good song ringing clear.

When the wind comes up from Cuba
And the birds are on the wing,
And our hearts are patting juba
To the banjo of the spring,

Then it's no wonder whether
The boys will get together,
With a stein on the table and a cheer for everything.

For we're all frank-and-twenty
When the spring is in the air;
And we've faith and hope a-plenty,
And we've life and love to spare;
And it's birds of a feather
When we all get together,
With a stein on the table and a heart without a care.

For we know the world is glorious,
And the goal a golden thing,
And that God is not censorious
When his children have their fling;
And life slips its tether
When the boys get together,
With a stein on the table in the fellowship of spring.

THE UNSAINTING OF KAVIN.

Saint Kavin was a gentleman,
He came from Tipperary;
And woman was the only thing
That ever made him scary.

For Kavin was a tender youth,
And he was very simple;
He feared the wiles of maiden smiles,
And fainted at a dimple.

But when Kathleen at seventeen
Came down the street one morning,
The luck of man came over him
And took him without warning.

Afraid to meet a foolish fate
By green sea or by dry land,
He fled away without delay
And sought a desert island.

But even there he felt despair;
For happiness is only
The hope of doing something else;
And he was very lonely.

He vowed to lead a life of prayer
Because that he had lost her;
And every time he thought of her
He said a *Pater noster*.

Yet hard it is for man to change
The less love for the greater;
And every time he reached *Amen*,
He must go back to *Pater*.

And so he grew a year or two
Disconsolate and holy,
While friends he'd known long since had grown
Papas and roly-poly.

Until one day, one blessed day,
A-moping like a Hindoo,
He saw Kathleen in mournful mien
A-passing by his window.

He threw away his rosary,
His *Paters* and his *Aves*;
For love is stronger than the wind
That wafts a thousand navies.

The holy man went forth to war,
But not against the devil.
He led the maid within for shade,
And treated her most civil.

He gave her cakes, he gave her wine,
He set his best before her;
And then invited her to dine--
Thenceforth--with her adorer.

Her little head went round for joy;
She tried to kick the rafter:

So Kavin was a saint no more,
And happy ever after.

IN THE WAYLAND WILLOWS.

Once I met a soncy maid,
Soncy maid, soncy maid,
Once I met a soncy maid
In the Wayland willows.

All her hair was goldy brown,
Goldy brown, goldy brown,
In the sun a single braid
To her waist hung down.

Honey bees, honey bees,
You are roving fellows!
Idly went the doxy wind
In the Wayland willows.

There I caught her eye a-dance,
Through the catkins downy.
"Heigho, Brownie-pate," said I;
"Heigho," said my Brownie.

Then I kissed my soncy maid,
Soncy maid, soncy maid,
Kissed and kissed my soncy maid
In the Wayland willows.

Goldy eyes and goldy hair,
And little gypsy bosom,
Chin and lip and shoulder tip,
Blossom after blossom!

Hand in hand and cheek by cheek
All the morning weather!
How the yellow butterflies
Danced and winked together!

Till the day went down the hill
Where the shadows waded.

"Heigho, Soncy!" "Heigho, me!"
Then I did as day did.

All her tousled beauty bright
And teasing as before,
I left her there in sweet despair,
A soncy maid no more.

WHEN I WAS TWENTY.

It was June, and I was twenty.
All my wisdom, poor but plenty,
Never learned Festina lente.
Youth is gone, but whither went he?

Madeline came down the orchard
With a mischief in her eye,
Half demure and half inviting,
Melting, wayward, wistful, shy.

Four bright eyes that found life lovely,
And forgot to wonder why;
Four warm lips at one love-lesson,
Learned by heart so easily.

We gained something of that knowledge
No man ever yet put by,
But his after days of sorrow
Left him nothing but to die.

Madeline went up the orchard,
Down the hurrying world went I;
Now I know love has no morrow,
Happiness no by-and-by.

Youth is gone, but whither went he?
All my wisdom, poor but plenty,
Never learned Festina lente.
It was June, and I was twenty.

IN A SILENCE.

Heart to heart!
And the stillness of night and the moonlight, like hushed breathing
Silently, stealthily moving across thy hair!

O womanly face!
Tender and strong and lucent with infinite feeling,
Shrinking with startled joy, like wind-struck water,
And yet so frank, so unashamed of love!

Ay, for there it is, love--that's the deepest.
Love's not love in the dark.
Light loves wither i' the sun, but Love endureth,
Clothing himself with the light as with a robe.

I would bare my soul to thy sight--
Leave not a secret deep unsearched,
Unrevealing its shame or its glory.
Love without Truth shall die as a soul without God.
A lying love is the love of a day
But the brave and true shall love forever.

Build Love a house;
Let the walls be thick;
Shut him in from the sight of men;
But hide not Love from himself.

Ah, the summer night!
The wind in the trees and the moonlight!
And my kisses on thy throat
And thy breathing in my hair!

Silent, lips to lips!
But our souls have held speech, thought answering echoing thought,
Though the only words were kisses.

THE BATHER.

I saw him go down to the water to bathe;
He stood naked upon the bank.

His breast was like a white cloud in the heaven,
that catches the sun;
It swelled with the sharp joy of the air.

His legs rose with the spring and curve of young birches;
The hollow of his back caught the blue shadows:

With his head thrown up to the lips of the wind;
And the curls of his forehead astir with the wind.

I would that I were a man, they are so beautiful;
Their bodies are like the bows of the Indians;
They have the spring and the grace of bows of hickory.

I know that women are beautiful, and that I am beautiful;
But the beauty of a man is so lithe and alive and triumphant,
Swift as the night of a swallow and sure as the
pounce of the eagle.

NOCTURNE: IN ANJOU

I dreamed of Sappho on a summer night.
Her nightingales were singing in the trees
Beside the castled river; and the wind
Fell like a woman's fingers on my cheek.
And then I slept and dreamed and marked no change;
The night went on with me into my dream.
This only I remember, that I cried:
"O Sappho! ere I leave this paradise,
Sing me one song of those lost books of yours
For which we poets still go sorrowing;
That when I meet my fellows on the earth
I may rejoice them more than many pearls;"
And she, the sweetly smiling, answered me,
As one who dreams, "I have forgotten them."

NOCTURNE: IN PROVENCE.

The blue night, like an angel, came into the room,--
Came through the open window from the silent sky
Down trellised stairs of moonlight into the dear room
As if a whisper breathed of some divine one nigh.
The nightingales, like brooks of song in Paradise,

Gurgled their serene rapture to the silent sky--
Like springs of laughter bubbling up in Paradise,
The serene nightingales along the riverside
Purled low in every tree their star-cool melodies
Of joy--in every tree along the riverside.

Did the vain garments melt in music from your side?
Did you rise from them as a lily flowers i' the air?
--But you were there before me like the Night's own bride--
I dared not call you mine. So still and tall you were,
I never dreamed that you were mine--I never dreamed
I loved you--I forgot I loved you. You were air
And music, and the shadows that you stood in, seemed
Like priests that keep their sombre vigil round a shrine--
Like sombre priests that watch about a glorious shrine.

And then you stepped into the moonlight and laid bare
The wonder of your body to the night, and stood
With all the stars of heaven looking at you there,
As simply as a saint might bare her soul to God--
As simply as a saint might bathe in lakes of prayer--
Stood with the holy moonlight falling on you there
Until I thought that in a glory unaware
I had seen a soul stand forth and bare itself to God--
A saintly soul lay bare its innocence to God.

JUNE NIGHT IN WASHINGTON.

The scent of honeysuckle,
Drugging the twilight
With its sweet opiate of lovers' dreams!
The last red glow of the setting sun
On the red brick wall
Of the neighboring house,
And the scramble of red roses over it!

Slowly, slowly
The night smokes up from the city to the stars,
The faint foreshadowed stars;
The smouldering night
Breathes upward like the breath
Of a woman asleep
With dim breast rising and falling
And a smile of delicate dreams.

Softly, softly
The wind comes into the garden,
Like a lover that fears lest he waken his love,
And his hands drip with the scent of the roses
And his locks weep with the opiate odor of honeysuckle.
Sighing, sighing
As a lover that yearns for the lips of his love,
In a torment of bliss,
In a passionate dreaming of bliss,
The wind in the trees of the garden!

How intimate are the trees,--
Rustling like the secret darkness of the soul!
How still is the starlight,--
Aloof in the placidity of dream!

Outside the garden
A group of negroes passing in the street
Sing with ripe lush voices,
Sing with voices that swim
Like great slow gliding fishes
Through the scent of the honeysuckle:

My love's waitin',
Waitin' by the river,
Waitin' till I come along!
Wait there, child; I'm comin'.

Jay-bird tol' me,
Tol' me in the mornin',
Tol' me she'd be there to-night.
Wait there, child; I'm comin'.

Waves of dream!
Spell of the summer night!
Will of the grass that stirs in its sleep!
Desire of the honeysuckle!
And further away,
Like the plash of far-off waves in the fluid night,
The negroes, singing:

Whip-po'-will tol' me,
Tol' me in the evenin',

"Down by the bend where the cat-tails grow."
Wait there, child; I'm comin'.

Lo, the moon,
Like a galleon sailing the night;
And the wash of the moonlight over the roofs and the trees!

Oh, my bride,
Come down from yonder lattice where you bide
Like a charmed princess in a Persian song!
I look up at your yellow window-panes,
Set in the night with far-off wizardry.
Come down, come down; the night is fain of you,
The garden waits your footstep on its walks.

Lo, the moon,
Like a galleon sailing the night;
And the wash of the moonlight over the red brick wall and the
roses!

A gleam of lamplight through an open door!
A footfall like the wind's upon the grass!
A rustle like the wind's among the leaves!...
Dim as a dream of pale peach blooms of light,
Blue in the blue soft pallor of the moon,
She comes between the trees as a faint tune
Falls from a flute far off into the night....
So Death might come to one who knew him Love.

A SONG FOR MARNA.

Dame of the night of hair
Like blue smoke blown!
World yet undreamed-of there
Lurks to be known.

Dame of the dizzy eyes,
Lure of dim quests!
World of what midnights lies
Under thy breasts!

Dame of the quench of love,
Give me to quaff!

There's all the world's made of
Under thy laugh.

Dame of the dare of gods,
Let the sky lower!
Time, give the world for odds,--
I choose this hour.

SEPTEMBER WOODLANDS.

This is not sadness in the wood;
The yellowbird
Flits joying through the solitude,
By no thought stirred
Save of his little duskier mate
And rompings jolly.

If there's a Dryad in the wood,
She is not sad.
Too wise the spirits are to brood;
Divinely glad,
They dream with countenance sedate
Not melancholy.

NANCIBEL.

The ghost of a wind came over the hill,
While day for a moment forgot to die,
And stirred the sheaves
Of the millet leaves,
As Nancibel went by.

Out of the lands of Long Ago,
Into the land of By and By,
Faded the gleam
Of a journeying dream,
As Nancibel went by.

THREE OF A KIND.

Three of us without a care
In the red September
Tramping down the roads of Maine,

Making merry with the rain,
With the fellow winds a-fare
Where the winds remember.

Three of us with shocking hats,
Tattered and unbarbered,
Happy with the splash of mud,
With the highways in our blood,
Bearing down on Deacon Platt's
Where last year we harbored.

We've come down from Kennebec,
Tramping since last Sunday,
Loping down the coast of Maine,
With the sea for a refrain,
And the maples neck and neck
All the way to Fundy.

Sometimes lodging in an inn,
Cosey as a dormouse--
Sometimes sleeping on a knoll
With no rooftree but the Pole--
Sometimes halely welcomed in
At an old-time farmhouse.

Loafing under ledge and tree,
Leaping over boulders,
Sitting on the pasture bars,
Hail-fellow with storm or stars--
Three of us alive and free,
With unburdened shoulders!

Three of us with hearts like pine
That the lightnings splinter,
Clean of cleave and white of grain--
Three of us afoot again,
With a rapture fresh and fine
As a spring in winter!

All the hills are red and gold;
And the horns of vision
Call across the crackling air
Till we shout back to them there,

Taken captive in the hold
Of their bluff derision.

Spray-salt gusts of ocean blow
From the rocky headlands;
Overhead the wild geese fly,
Honking in the autumn sky;
Black sinister flocks of crow
Settle on the dead lands.

Three of us in love with life,
Roaming like wild cattle,
With the stinging air a-reel
As a warrior might feel
The swift orgasm of the knife
Slay him in mid-battle.

Three of us to march abreast
Down the hills of morrow!
With a clean heart and a few
Friends to clench the spirit to!--
Leave the gods to rule the rest,
And good-by, sorrow!

WOOD-FOLK LORE.TO T. B. M.

For every one
Beneath the sun,
Where Autumn walks with quiet eyes,
There is a word,
Just overheard
When hill to purple hill replies.

This afternoon,
As warm as June,
With the red apples on the bough,
I set my ear
To hark and hear
The wood-folk talking, you know how.

There comes a "Hush!"
And then a "Tush,"
As tree to scarlet tree responds,
"Babble away!

He'll not betray
The secrets of us vagabonds.

"Are we not all,
Both great and small,
Cousins and kindred in a joy
No school can teach,
No worldling reach,
Nor any wreck of chance destroy?"

And so we are,
However far
We journey ere the journey ends,
One brotherhood
With leaf and bud
And everything that wakes or wends.

The wind that blows
My autumn rose
Where Grand Pré looks to Blomidon,--
How great must be
The company
Of roses he has leaned upon,

Since first he shed
Their petals red
Through Persian gardens long ago,
When Omar heard
His muttered word
Rumoring things we may not know!

Our brother ghost,
He is a most
Incorrigible wanderer;
And still to-day
He takes his way
About my hills of spruce and fir;

Will neither bide
By the great tide,
In apple lands of Acadie,
Nor in the leaves
About your eaves,
Where Scituate looks out to sea.

AT MICHAELMAS.

About the time of Michael's feast
And all his angels,
There comes a word to man and beast
By dark evangels.

Then hearing what the wild things say
To one another,
Those creatures first born of our gray
Mysterious Mother,

The greatness of the world's unrest
Steals through our pulses;
Our own life takes a meaning guessed
From the torn dulse's.

The draft and set of deep sea-tides
Swirling and flowing,
Bears every filmy flake that rides,
Grandly unknowing.

The sunlight listens; thin and fine
The crickets whistle;
And floating midges fill the shine
Like a seeding thistle.

The hawkbit flies his golden flag
From rocky pasture,
Bidding his legions never lag
Through morning's vasture.

Soon we shall see the red vines ramp
Through forest borders,
And Indian summer breaking camp
To silent orders.

The glossy chestnuts swell and burst
Their prickly houses
Agog at news which reached them first
In sap's carouses.

The long noons turn the ribstons red,
The pippins yellow;
The wild duck from his reedy bed
Summons his fellow.

The robins keep the underbrush
Songless and wary,
As though they feared some frostier hush
Might bid them tarry;

Perhaps in the great North they heard
Of silence falling
Upon the world without a word,
White and appalling.

The ash-tree and the lady-fern,
In russet frondage,
Proclaim 'tis time for our return
To vagabondage.

All summer idle have we kept;
But on a morning,
Where the blue hazy mountains slept,
A scarlet warning

Disturbs our day-dream with a start;
A leaf turns over;
And every earthling is at heart
Once more a rover.

All winter we shall toil and plod,
Eating and drinking;
But now's the little time when God
Sets folk to thinking.

"Consider," says the quiet sun,
"How far I wander;
Yet when had I not time on one
More flower to squander?"

"Consider," says the restless tide,
"My endless labor;

Yet when was I content beside
My nearest neighbor?"

So wander-lust to wander-lure,
As seed to season
Must rise and wend, possessed and sure
In sweet unreason.

For doorstone and repose are good,
And kind is duty;
But joy is in the solitude
With shy-heart beauty.

And Truth is one whose ways are meek
Beyond foretelling;
And far his journey who would seek
Her lowly dwelling.

She leads him by a thousand heights,
Lonelily faring,
With sunrise and with eagle flights
To mate his daring.

For her he fronts a vaster fog
Than Leif of yore did,
Voyaging for continents no log
Has yet recorded.

He travels by a polar star,
Now bright, now hidden,
For a free land, though rest be far
And roads forbidden,

Till on a day with sweet coarse bread
And wine she stays him,
Then in a cool and narrow bed
To slumber lays him.

So we are hers. And, fellows mine
Of fin and feather,
By shady wood and shadowy brine,
When comes the weather

For migrants to be moving on,
By lost indenture
You flock and gather and are gone:
The old adventure!

I too have my unwritten date,
My gypsy presage;
And on the brink of fall I wait
The darkling message.

The sign, from prying eyes concealed,
Is yet how flagrant!
Here's ragged-robin in the field,
A simple vagrant.

THE MOTHER OF POETS. TO H. F. H.

The typewriter ticketh no more in the twilight;
The mother of poets is sitting alone;
Only the katydid teases the noonday;
Where are the good-for-naught wanderbirds flown?

Tom's in the North with his purple impressions;
Dickon's in London a-building his fame;
Fred's in the mountains a-minding his cattle;
Kavanagh's teaching and preaching and game.

Over in Kingscroft a toiler is writing,
The boyish Old Man whom no fate ever floored;
Karl's in New York with his briefs and his logic,
That subtile mind like a velvet-sheathed sword.

Blomidon welcomes his brother in silence;
Grand Pré is luring him back to her breast;
Faint and far off are the cries of the city,
There in the country of infinite rest.

All of them turn in their wide vagabondage,
Halt and remember a place they have known,
Where the typewriter ticketh no more in the twilight,
And the mother of poets is sitting alone.

There they will surely some April forgather,
Drink once together before they depart,
One by one over the threshold of silence,
On the long trail of the wandering heart.

Fear not, little mother, there may be a region
Where poets have only to smile and keep still.
The tick of the typewriter there will be useless,
But there will be need of a motherkin still.

A GOOD-BY.

For love of the roving foot
And joy of the roving eye,
God send you store of morrows fair
And a good rest by and by!

IN A COPY OF BROWNING.

Browning, old fellow,
Your leaves grow yellow,
Beginning to mellow
As seasons pass.
Your cover is wrinkled,
And stained and sprinkled,
And warped and crinkled
From sleep on the grass.

Is it a wine stain,
Or only a pine stain,
That makes such a fine stain
On your dull blue,--
Got as we numbered
The clouds that lumbered
Southward and slumbered
When day was through?

What is the dear mark
There like an earmark,
Only a tear mark
A woman let fall?--
As bending over
She bade me discover,

"Who *plays* the lover,
He loses all!"

With you for teacher
We learned love's feature
In every creature
That roves or grieves;
When winds were brawling,
Or bird-folk calling,
Or leaf-folk falling,
About our eaves.

No law must straiten
The ways they wait in,
Whose spirits greaten
And hearts aspire.
The world may dwindle,
And summer brindle,
So love but kindle
The soul to fire.

Here many a red line,
Or pencilled headline,
Shows love could wed line
To golden sense;
And something better
Than wisdom's fetter
Has made your letter
Dense to the dense.

No April robin,
Nor clacking bobbin,
Can make of Dobbin
A Pegasus;
But Nature's pleading
To man's unheeding,
Your subtile reading
Made clear to us.

You made us farers
And equal sharers
With homespun wearers
In home-made joys;
You made us princes

No plea convinces
That spirit winces
At dust and noise.

When Fate was nagging,
And days were dragging,
And fancy lagging,
You gave it scope,--
When eaves were drippy,
And pavements slippy,--
From Lippo Lippi
To Evelyn Hope.

When winter's arrow
Pierced to the marrow,
And thought was narrow,
You gave it room;
We guessed the warder
On Roland's border,
And helped to order
The Bishop's Tomb.

When winds were harshish,
And ways were marshish,
We found with Karshish
Escape at need;
Were bold with Waring
In far seafaring,
And strong in snaring
Ben Ezra's creed.

We felt the menace
Of lovers pen us,
Afloat in Venice
Devising fibs;
And little mattered
The rain that pattered,
While Blougram chattered
To Gigadibs.

And we too waited
With heart elated
And breathing bated,
For Pippa's song;

Saw Satan hover,
With wings to cover
Porphyria's lover,
Pompilia's wrong.

Long thoughts were started,
When youth departed
From the half-hearted
Riccardi's bride;
For, saith your fable,
Great Love is able
To slip the cable
And take the tide.

Or truth compels us
With Paracelsus,
Till nothing else is
Of worth at all.
Del Sarto's vision
Is our own mission,
And art's ambition
Is God's own call.

Through all the seasons,
You gave us reasons
For splendid treasons
To doubt and fear;
Bade no foot falter,

Though weaklings palter,
And friendships alter
From year to year.

Since first I sought you,
Found you and bought you,
Hugged you and brought you
Home from Cornhill,
While some upbraid you,
And some parade you,
Nine years have made you
My master still.

SHAKESPEARE HIMSELF: FOR THE UNVEILING OF MR. PARTRIDGE'S STATUE OF THE POET.

The body is no prison where we lie
Shut out from our true heritage of sun;
It is the wings wherewith the soul may fly.
Save through this flesh so scorned and spat upon,
No ray of light had reached the caverned mind,
No thrill of pleasure through the life had run,
No love of nature or of humankind,
Were it but love of self, had stirred the heart
To its first deed. Such freedom as we find,
We find but through its service, not apart.
And as an eagle's wings upbear him higher
Than Andes or Himalaya, and chart
Rivers and seas beneath; so our desire,
With more celestial members yet, may soar
Into the space of empyrean fire,
Still bodied but more richly than before.

The body is the man; what lurks behind
Through it alone unveils itself. Therefore
We are not wrong, who seek to keep in mind
The form and feature of the mighty dead.
So back of all the giving is divined
The giver, back of all things done or said
The man himself in elemental speech
Of flesh and bone and sinew utterèd.

This is thy language, Sculpture. Thine to reach
Beneath all thoughts, all feelings, all desires,
To that which thinks and lives and loves, and teach
The world the primal selfhood of its sires,
Its heroes and its lovers and its gods.
So shall Apollo flame in marble fires,
The mien of Zeus suffice before he nods,
So Gautama in ivory dream out
The calm of Time's untrammelled periods,
So Sigurd's lips be in themselves a shout.

Mould us our Shakespeare, sculptor, in the form
His comrades knew, rare Ben and all the rout
That found the taproom of the Mermaid warm
With wit and wine and fellowship, the face
Wherein the men he chummed with found a charm
To make them love him; carve for us the grace
That caught Anne Hathaway in Shottery-side,
The hand that clasped Southampton's in the days

Ere that dark dame, of passion and of pride
Burned in his heart the brand of her disdain,
The eyes that wept when little Hamnet died,
The lips that learned from Marlowe's and again
Taught riper lore to Fletcher and the rest,
The presence and demeanor sovereign
At last at Stratford calm and manifest,
That rested on the seventh day and scanned
His work and knew it good, and left the quest
And like his own enchanter broke his wand.

No viewless mind! The very shape, no less,
He used to speak and smile with, move and stand!
God is most God not in his loneliness,
Unfellowed, discreationed, unrevealed,
Nor thundering on Sinai, pitiless,
Nor when the seven vials are unsealed,
But when his spirit companions with our thought
And in his fellowship our pain is healed;
And we are likest God when we are brought
Most near to all men. Bring us near to him,
The gentle, human soul whose calm might wrought
Imperious Lear and made our eyes grow dim
For Imogen,--who, though he heard the spheres
"Still choiring to the young-eyed cherubim,"
Could laugh with Falstaff and his loose compeers
And love the rascal with the same big heart
That o'er Cordelia could not stay its tears.

For still the man is greater than his art.
And though thy men and women, Shakespeare, rise
Like giants in our fancy and depart,
Thyself art more than all their masteries,
Thy wisdom more than Hamlet's questionings
Or the cold searching of Ulysses' eyes,
Thy mirth more sweet than Benedick's flouts and flings,
Thy smiling dearer than Mercutio's,
Thy dignity past that of all thy kings,
And thy enchantment more than Prospero's.

For thou couldst not have had Othello's flaw,
Not erred with Brutus,--greater, then, than those
For all their nobleness. Oh, albeit with awe,
Leave we the mighty phantoms and draw near
The man that fashioned them and gave them law!

The Master Poet found with scarce a peer
In all the ages his domain to share,
Yet of all singers gentlest and most dear!
Oh, how shall words thy proper praise declare,
Divine in thy supreme humanity
And near as the inevitable air?

So he that wrought this image deemed of thee;
So I, thy lover, keep thee in my heart;
So may this figure set for men to see
Where the world passes eager for the mart,
Be as a sudden insight of the soul
That makes a darkness into order start,
And lift thee up for all men, fair and whole,
Till scholar, merchant farmer, artisan,
Seeing, divine beneath the aureole
The fellow heart and know thee for a man.

AT THE ROAD-HOUSE: IN MEMORY OF ROBERT LOUIS STEVENSON.

You hearken, fellows? Turned aside
Into the road-house of the past!
The prince of vagabonds is gone
To house among his peers at last.

The stainless gallant gentleman,
So glad of life, he gave no trace,
No hint he even once beheld
The spectre peering in his face;

But gay and modest held the road,
Nor feared the Shadow of the Dust;
And saw the whole world rich with joy,
As every valiant farer must.

I think that old and vasty inn
Will have a welcome guest to-night,
When Chaucer, breaking off some tale
That fills his hearers with delight,

Shall lift up his demure brown eyes
To bid the stranger in; and all

Will turn to greet the one on whom
The crystal lot was last to fall.

Keats of the more than mortal tongue
Will take grave Milton by the sleeve
To meet their kin, whose woven words
Had elvish music in the weave.

Dear Lamb and excellent Montaigne,
Sterne and the credible Defoe,
Borrow, DeQuincey, the great Dean,
The sturdy leisurist Thoreau;

The furtive soul whose dark romance,
By ghostly door and haunted stair,
Explored the dusty human heart
And the forgotten garrets there;

The moralist it could not spoil,
To hold an empire in his hands;
Sir Walter, and the brood who sprang
From Homer through a hundred lands,

Singers of songs on all men's lips,
Tellers of tales in all men's ears,
Movers of hearts that still must beat
To sorrows feigned and fabled tears;

Horace and Omar, doubting still
What mystery lurks beyond the seen,
Yet blithe and reassured before
That fine unvexed Virgilian mien;

These will companion him to-night,
Beyond this iron wintry gloom,
When Shakespeare and Cervantes bid
The great joy-masters give him room.

No alien there in speech or mood,
He will pass in, one traveller more;
And portly Ben will smile to see
The velvet jacket at the door.

VERLAINE.

Avid of life and love, insatiate vagabond,
With quest too furious for the graal he would have won,
He flung himself at the eternal sky, as one
Wrenching his chains but impotent to burst the bond.

Yet under the revolt, the revel, the despond,
What pools of innocence, what crystal benison!
As through a riven mist that glowers in the sun,
A stretch of God's blue calm glassed in a virgin pond.

Prowler of obscene streets that riot reek along,
And aisles with incense numb and gardens mad with rose,
Monastic cells and dreams of dim brocaded lawns,

Death, which has set the calm of Time upon his song,
Surely upon his soul has kissed the same repose
In some fair heaven the Christ has set apart for Fauns.

DISTILLATION.

They that eat the uncrushed grape
Walk with steady heels:
Lo, now, how they stare and gape
Where the poet reels!
He has drunk the sheer divine
Concentration of the vine.

A FRIEND'S WISH. TO C. W. S.

Give me your last *Aloha*,
When I go out of sight,
Over the dark rim of the sea
Into the Polar night!

And all the Northland give you
Skoal for the voyage begun,
When your bright summer sail goes down
Into the zones of sun!

LAL OF KILRUDDEN.

Kilrudden ford, Kilrudden dale,
Kilrudden fronting every gale
On the lorn coast of Inishfree,
And Lal's last bed the plunging sea.

Lal of Kilrudden with flame-red hair,
And the sea-blue eyes that rove and dare,
And the open heart with never a care;
With her strong brown arms and her ankles bare,
God in heaven, but she was fair,
That night the storm put in from sea?

The nightingales of Inishkill,
The rose that climbed her window-sill,
The shade that rustled or was still,
The wind that roved and had his will,
And one white sail on the low sea-hill,
Were all she knew of love.

So when the storm drove in that day,
And her lover's ship on the ledges lay,
Past help and wrecking in the gray,
And the cry was, "Who'll go down the bay,
With half of the lifeboat's crew away?"
Who should push to the front and say,
"I will be one, be others who may,"
But Lal of Kilrudden, born at sea!

The nightingales all night in the rain,
The rose that fell at her window-pane,
The frost that blackened the purple plain,
And the scorn of pitiless disdain
At the hands of the wolfish pirate main,
Quelling her great hot heart in vain,
Were all she knew of death.

Kilrudden ford, Kilrudden dale,
Kilrudden ruined in the gale
That wrecked the coast of Inishfree,
And Lal's last bed the plunging sea.

HUNTING-SONG: FROM "KING ARTHUR."

Oh, who would stay indoor, indoor,
When the horn is on the hill? (*Bugle:* Tarantara!
With the crisp air stinging, and the huntsmen singing,
And a ten-tined buck to kill!

Before the sun goes down, goes down,
We shall slay the buck of ten; (*Bugle:* Tarantara!
And the priest shall say benison, and we shall ha'e venison,
When we come home again.

Let him that loves his ease, his ease,
Keep close and house him fair; (*Bugle:* Tarantara!
He'll still be a stranger to the merry thrill of danger
And the joy of the open air.

But he that loves the hills, the hills,
Let him come out to-day! (*Bugle:*Tarantara!
For the horses are neighing, and the hounds are baying,
And the hunt's up, and away!

BUIE ANNAJOHN.

Buie Annajohn was the king's black mare,
Buie, Buie, Buie Annajohn!
Satin was her coat and silk was her hair,
Buie Annajohn,
The young king's own.
March with the white moon, march with the sun,
March with the merry men, Buie Annajohn!

Buie Annajohn, when the dew lay hoar,
(Buie, Buie, Buie Annajohn!)
Down through the meadowlands went to war,--
Buie Annajohn,
The young king's own.
March by the river road, march by the dune,
March with the merry men, Buie Annajohn!

Buie Annajohn had the heart of flame,
Buie, Buie, Buie Annajohn!
First of the hosts to the hostings came
Buie Annajohn,
The young king's own.

March till we march the red sun down,
March with the merry men, Buie Annajohn!

Back from the battle at the close of day,
(Buie, Buie, Buie Annajohn!)
Came with the war cheers, came with a neigh,
Buie Annajohn,
The young king's own.
Oh, heavy was the sword that we laid on;
But half of the heave was Buie Annajohn,
Buie, Buie, Buie Annajohn!

MARY OF MARKA.

Eric of Marka holds the knife:
"A nameless death for a nameless life."--

"Mary of Marka, bid him stay,
And the morrow shall be our wedding-day."--

"Will the blessing of priest give back my faith,
Or life to the child you left to death?"--

Eric of Marka holds the knife,
And turns to the mother that is no wife:

"Mary of Marka, have your will!
Shall I spare him, or shall I kill?"--

"He wrought me wrong when the days were sweet,
And he'll get no more but a winding-sheet."

PREMONITION.

He said, "Good-night, my heart is light,
To-morrow morn at day
We two together in the dew
Shall forth and fare away.

"We shall go down, the halls of dawn
To find the doors of joy;
We shall not part again, dear heart."
And he laughed out like a boy.

He turned and strode down the blue road
Against the western sky
Where the last line of sunset glowed
As sullen embers die.

The night reached out her kraken arms
To clutch him as he passed,
And for one sudden moment
My soul shrank back aghast.

THE HEARSE-HORSE.

Said the hearse-horse to the coffin,
"What the devil have you there?
I may trot from court to square,
Yet it neither swears nor groans,
When I jolt it over stones."
Said the coffin to the hearse-horse,
"Bones!"

Said the hearse-horse to the coffin,
"What the devil have you there,
With that purple frozen stare?
Where the devil has it been
To get that shadow grin?"
Said the coffin to the hearse-horse,
"Skin!"

Said the hearse-horse to the coffin,
"What the devil have you there?
It has fingers, it has hair;
Yet it neither kicks nor squirms
At the undertaker's terms."
Said the coffin to the hearse-horse,
"Worms!"

THE NIGHT-WASHERS.

Whe-ooh, ooh, ooh, ooh, ooh!
We are the brothers of ghouls, and who
In the name of the Crooked Saints are you?

We are the washers of shrouds wherein
The lovers of beauty who sainted sin
Sleep till the Judgment Day begin.

When the moon is drifting overhead,
We wash the linen of the dead,
Stained with yellow and stiff with red.

Whe-ooh, ooh, ooh, ooh, ooh!
We are the foul night-washers, and who,
By the Seven Lovely sins are you?

Here we sit by the river reeds,
Rinsing the linen that reeks and bleeds,
And craving the help our labor needs.

Come, Sir Fop, fall to, fall to!
Show us for once what you can do!
One day there'll be washing enough for you.

Wade in, wade in, where the river runs
Clear in the moonlight over the stones!
It'll wash the ache from your scrofulous bones.

Whe-ooh, ooh, ooh, ooh, ooh!
We are the gossips of fame, and who
By the Sinners' Litany are you?

Wade in, wade in! The water is cold,
The stains are deep, and the linen is old;
But surely the sons of the town are bold!

Work for us here till the break of day
At washing the stains of the dead away,
And you shall be merry, come what may!

From now till your ninetieth year begins,
You shall sin the Seven Lovely sins,
While wearing the virtue a cardinal wins.

Refuse, and your arms shall be broken and wried,
To dangle like fenders over the side
Of an empty ship on the harbor tide!

They shall gather a waist in their grip no more,
As you wander the wide world over and o'er,
With the curs at your heels from door to door.

With only a stranger to cover your face,
You shall die in the streets of an outcast race,
And your linen be washed in the market-place!

Whe-ooh, ooh, ooh, ooh, ooh!
We are the Scavenger Saints, but who
In the name of the Shadowy Kin are you?

MR. MOON: A SONG OF THE LITTLE PEOPLE.

O Moon, Mr. Moon,
When you comin' down?
Down on the hilltop,
Down in the glen,
Out in the clearin',
To play with little men?
Moon, Mr. Moon,
When you comin' down?

O Mr. Moon,
Hurry up your stumps!
Don't you hear Bullfrog
Callin' to his wife,
And old black Cricket
A-wheezin' at his fife?
Hurry up your stumps,
And get on your pumps!
Moon, Mr. Moon,
When you comin' down?

O Mr. Moon,
Hurry up along!
The reeds in the current
Are whisperin' slow;
The river's a-wimplin'
To and fro.
Or you'll miss the song!
Moon, Mr. Moon,
When you comin' down?

O Mr. Moon,
We're all here!
Honey-bug, Thistledrift,
White-imp, Weird,
Wryface, Billiken,
Quidnunc, Queered;
We're all here,
And the coast is clear!
Moon, Mr. Moon,
When you comin' down?

O Mr. Moon,
We're the little men!
Dewlap, Pussymouse,
Ferntip, Freak,
Drink-again, Shambler,
Talkytalk, Squeak;
Three times ten
Of us little men!
Moon, Mr. Moon,
When you comin' down?

O Mr. Moon,
We're all ready!
Tallenough, Squaretoes,
Amble, Tip,
Buddybud, Heigho,
Little black Pip;
We're all ready,
And the wind walks steady!
Moon, Mr. Moon,
When you comin' down?

O Mr. Moon,
We're thirty score;
Yellowbeard, Piper,
Lieabed, Toots,
Meadowbee, Moonboy,
Bully-in-boots;
Three times more
Than thirty score.
Moon, Mr. Moon,
When you comin' down?

O Mr. Moon,
Keep your eye peeled;
Watch out to windward,
Or you'll miss the fun,
Down by the acre
Where the wheat-waves run;
Keep your eye peeled
For the open field.
Moon, Mr. Moon,
When you comin' down?

O Mr. Moon,
There's not much time!
Hurry, if you're comin',
You lazy old bones!
You can sleep to-morrow
While the Buzbuz drones;
There's not much time
Till the church bells chime.
Moon, Mr. Moon,
When you comin' down?

O Mr. Moon,
Just see the clover!
Soon we'll be going
Where the Gray Goose went
When all her money
Was spent, spent, spent!
Down through the clover,
When the revel's over!
Moon, Mr. Moon,
When you comin' down?

O Moon, Mr. Moon,
When you comin' down?
Down where the Good Folk
Dance in a ring,
Down where the Little Folk
Sing?
Moon, Mr. Moon,
When you comin' down?

HEM AND HAW.

Hem and Haw were the sons of sin,
Created to shally and shirk;
Hem lay 'round and Haw looked on
While God did all the work.

Hem was a fogy, and Haw was a prig,
For both had the dull, dull mind;
And whenever they found a thing to do,
They yammered and went it blind.

Hem was the father of bigots and bores;
As the sands of the sea were they.
And Haw was the father of all the tribe
Who criticise to-day.

But God was an artist from the first,
And knew what be was about;
While over his shoulder sneered these two,
And advised him to rub it out.

They prophesied ruin ere man was made:
"Such folly must surely fail!"
And when he was done, "Do you think, my Lord,
He's better without a tail?"

And still in the honest working world,
With posture and hint and smirk,
These sons of the devil are standing by
While Man does all the work.

They balk endeavor and baffle reform,
In the sacred name of law;
And over the quavering voice of Hem
Is the droning voice of Haw.

ACCIDENT IN ART.

That painter has not with a careless smutch
Accomplished his despair?--one touch revealing
All he had put of life, thought, vigor, feeling,
Into the canvas that without that touch
Showed of his love and labor just so much
Raw pigment, scarce a scrap of soul concealing!

What poet has not found his spirit kneeling
A sudden at the sound of such or such
Strange verses staring from his manuscript,
Written he knows not how, but which will sound
Like trumpets down the years? So Accident
Itself unmasks the likeness of Intent,
And ever in blind Chance's darkest crypt
The shrine-lamp of God's purposing is found.

IN A GARDEN.

Thought is a garden wide and old
For airy creatures to explore,
Where grow the great fantastic flowers
With truth for honey at the core.

There like a wild marauding bee
Made desperate by hungry fears,
From gorgeous *If* to dark *Perhaps*
I blunder down the dusk of years.

AT THE END OF THE DAY.

There is no escape by the river,
There is no flight left by the fen;
We are compassed about by the shiver
Of the night of their marching men.
Give a cheer!
For our hearts shall not give way.
Here's to a dark to-morrow,
And here's to a brave to-day!

The tale of their hosts is countless,
And the tale of ours a score;
But the palm is naught to the dauntless,
And the cause is more and more.
Give a cheer!
We may die, but not give way.
Here's to a silent morrow,
And here's to a stout to-day!

God has said: "Ye shall fail and perish;
But the thrill ye have felt to-night
I shall keep in my heart and cherish

When the worlds have passed in night."
Give a cheer!
For the soul shall not give way.
Here's to the greater to-morrow
That is born of a great to-day!

Now shame on the craven truckler
And the puling things that mope!
We've a rapture for our buckler
That outwears the wings of hope.
Give a cheer!
For our joy shall not give way.
Here's in the teeth of to-morrow
To the glory of to-day!

THIS BOOK WAS PRINTED BY JOHN WILSON AND SON, AT
THE UNIVERSITY PRESS, CAMBRIDGE, MASSACHUSETTS,
DURING OCTOBER,
1896.

LAST SONGS FROM VAGABONDIA

BLISS CARMAN RICHARD HOVEY

AT THE CROSSROADS

YOU to the left and I to the right,
For the ways of men must sever—
And it well may be for a day and a night,
And it well may be forever.
But whether we meet or whether we part   5
(For our ways are past our knowing),
A pledge from the heart to its fellow heart
On the ways we all are going!
Here's luck!
For we know not where we are going.   10

We have striven fair in love and war,
But the wheel was always weighted;
We have lost the prize that we struggled for,
We have won the prize that was fated.
We have met our loss with a smile and a song,   15
And our gains with a wink and a whistle,—
For, whether we're right or whether we're wrong.
There's a rose for every thistle.
Here's luck—
And a drop to wet your whistle!   20

Whether we win or whether we lose
With the hands that life is dealing,
It is not we nor the ways we choose
But the fall of the cards that's sealing.
There's a fate in love and a fate in fight,   25
And the best of us all go under—
And whether we're wrong or whether we're right,
We win, sometimes, to our wonder.
Here's luck—
That we may not yet go under!   30

With a steady swing and an open brow
We have tramped the ways together,
But we're clasping hands at the crossroads now
In the Fiend's own night for weather;
And whether we bleed or whether we smile   35

In the leagues that lie before us,
The ways of life are many a mile
And the dark of Fate is o'er us.
Here's luck!
And a cheer for the dark before us!   40

You to the left and I to the right,
For the ways of men must sever,
And it well may be for a day and a night,
And it well may be forever!
But whether we live or whether we die   45
(For the end is past our knowing),
Here's two frank hearts and the open sky,
Be a fair or an ill wind blowing!
Here's luck!
In the teeth of all winds blowing.   50

"AT LAST, O DEATH!"

AT last, O death!
Not with the sick-room fever and weary heart
And slow subsidence of diminished breath—
But strong and free
With the great tumult of the living sea.   5
Behold, I have loved.
And though I wept for the long sundering,
I did not fear thee, Death, nor then nor now.
I girded up my loins and sought my kind,
And did a man's work in a world of men,   10
And looked upon my work and called it good.
Now come, then, in the shape I love the best.
In the salt, sturdy wrestling of the sea,
I give thee welcome

MAY AND JUNE

MAY comes, day comes,
One who was away comes;
All the earth is glad again,
Kind and fair to me.
May comes, day comes,   5
One who was away comes;
Set his place at hearth and board   10

As they used to be.
May comes, day comes,
One who was away comes;
Higher are the hills of home,
Bluer is the sea.

II

June comes, and the moon comes
Out of the curving sea,
Like a frail golden bubble,   15
To hang in the lilac tree.
June comes, and a croon comes
Up from the old gray sea,
But not the longed-for footstep
And the voice at the door for me.   20

PHILIP SAVAGE

FIELDS by Massachusetts Bay,
Where is he who yesterday
Called you Home, and loved to go
Where the cherry spreads her snow,
Through the purple misty woods   5
Of your soft spring solitudes,
Listening for the first fine gush
Of his fellow, the shy thrush—
Hearkening some diviner tone
Than our ears have ever known?   10

Woodland-musing by the hour
When the locust comes in flower,
He would watch by hill and swamp
Every sign of her green pomp
Where your matchless June once more   15
Leads her pageant up the shore.
Slopes of bayberry and fern,
While you wait for his return,
Can it be that he would test
Some far region of the West,   20

Tracking some great river course
To its undiscovered source?
Or an idler would he be
In the Islands of the Sea?
Can it be that he is gone,   25

Like so many a roving one,
The dread Arctic to explore,
Never to be heard of more—
Or with those who sail away
Every year from Gloucester Bay

30

For the Banks, and do not come
When the fishing fleets come home?
Stony uplands where the quail
Whistles by the pasture rail,
Where is one to whom you lent

35

Of your wise serene content,
Minstrel of your pagan psalm
With an Emersonian calm?
Open fields along the sea,
'T was your sweet sincerity

40

Made him what his fellows knew,
Sober, gentle, sane and true.
Whippoorwill and oriole,
He had your untarnished soul;
He your steadfast brother was,

45

Lowly field-bird of the grass.
Shores of Massachusetts Bay,
Teach us only in our day
Half as well your face to love
And your loving kindness prove.

50

Now the wind he loved so well
Makes the dune grass rock and swell,
And the marshy acres run
White with charlock in the sun,
Should he not be here to see

55

All your brave felicity!
Through these orchards green and dim,
Whose old calm was good to him,
Let the tiny yellow birds
Still repeat their shining words,

60

While across our senses steal
Hints of things no words reveal.
Let the air he used to know
From the iris meadows blow,
At evening through the open door

65

With the cool scents of the shore,
While across our spirits sweep
Sea-turns from a vaster deep.
Sunlit fields, how gently now
Your white daisies nod and bow,   70

Where the soft wind and the sun
Grieve not for a mortal one!
Only the old sea the more
Seems to whisper and deplore,
Murmuring like a childless crone   75
With her sorrow left alone—
The eternal human cry
To the heedless passer by.
Marshes, while your channels fill
And the June birds have their will,   80

While the elms along your edge
Wave above the rusty sedge,
And the bobolinks day long
Ply their juggleries of song,
While the sailing ships go by   85
To their ports below the sky,
Still the old Thalassian blue
Bounds this lovely world for you,
And the lost horizon lies
Past your wonder or surmise.   90

Fields by Massachusetts Bay,
When your questioner shall say,
"Where is he who should have been
Poet of your lovely mien,
And your soul's interpreter?"   95
Answer, every larch and fir,
"He was here, but he is gone.
Some high purpose not his own
Summoned his unwasted powers
From our common woods and flowers.   100

All too soon from our abode
Back he wended to the road,
Rich in love, if not in fame.
Philip Savage was his name."

NON OMNIS MORIAR

THIS paragraph cannot be true;
For such a man could not have died.
Death is so lonely, hard and cold,—
Not gentleness personified.
What manner was it in the man   5
That makes the story seem untrue?
Death is for fighters, rakes, and kings;
Malice nor greed he never knew.
He never seemed to strive to live;
His spirit was too sure for strife,—   10
Too glad, unquerulous and fair,
To take the sordid tinge of life.
The pompous folly of the world
Could never touch that radiant mien;
He moved unstained among the crowd,   15
Loyal, courageous, and serene.
No bargainer for wealth nor fame
Nor place, his was a better part,—
The simple love of all his kind,
And lifelong fervour in his art.   20

It must have been his charity,
That tender human heart of his,
That rare unfailing kindliness,
Could make his death seem so amiss.
In London where he lived and toiled,   25
I saw him smile across the throng,
The unembittered smile of those
Whose sweetness triumphs over wrong.
With that unvexed Chaucerian mood,
That zest unsevered from repose,   30
He is as wise as Omar now,
Or any Master of the Rose.
And here in the November dusk
There comes an echo, faint and far,
Of that gay, valiant, careless voice   35
That cried, Non omnis moriar!
Behind the mask of lore and creed
There dwells an instinct, strong and blind,
Refuting sorrow, bidding grief
Be something better than resigned.   40

There is a part of me that knows,
Beneath incertitude and fear,
I shall not perish when I pass
Beyond mortality's frontier;
But greatly having joyed and grieved,   45
Greatly content, shall hear the sigh
Of the strange wind across the lone
Bright lands of taciturnity.
In patience therefore I await
My friend's unchanged benign regard,—   50
Some April when I too shall be
Split water from a broken shard.

THE CITY IN THE SEA

ONCE of old there stood a fabled city
By the Breton sea,
Towered and belled and flagged and wreathed and
pennoned
For the pomp of Yuletide revelry;
All its folk, adventurous, sea-daring,   5
Gay as gay could be.
And at night when window, torch, and bonfire
Lighted up the sky,
Down the wind came galleon and pinnace,
Steered for that red lantern, riding high;   10
Every brown hand hard upon the tiller,
Shore ward every eye.
Well I see that hardy Breton sailor
With the bearded lip,—
How he laughed out, holding his black racer   15
Where the travelling sea-hills climb and slip,
Chased by storm and lighted on to haven,
Ship by homing ship.
Every sail came in, like deep-sea rovers
Who have heard afar   20
Wild and splendid hyperborean rumours
Of a respite made to feud and war,—
Making port where sea-wreck and disaster
Should not vex them more.
What of Ys? Where was it when gray morning   25
Gloomed o'er Brittany?
Smothered out in elemental fury,   30

Wrecked and whelmed in the engulfing sea,
To become the name of a sea-story
In lost legendry.

In my heart there is a sunken city,
Wonderful as Ys.
All day long I hear the mellow tolling
Of its sweet-sad lonely bells of peace,
Rocked by tides that wash through all its portals   35
Without let or cease.
Pale and fitful as the wan auroras
Are its nights and days;
In from nowhere flush the drafty sea-turns
By forgotten and neglected ways;   40
Through the entries and the doors of being
That faint music strays;
Tolling back the wandered and the way-worn
From far alien lands;
Tolling back the gipsy child of beauty   45
With mysterious and soft commands;
Tolling back the spirit that within me
Hears and understands.
Then some May night, with a scent of lilacs
In the magic air,   50
Through the moonlight and the mad spring weather,
(Old love's fervour and new love's despair),
I go down to my familiar city,
Roaming court and square.
Of a sudden at a well-known corner,   55
In the densest throng,
Unexpected at the very moment
As an April robin's gush of song,
Some one smiles; and there's the perfect comrade
I have missed so long.   60

Then, at just the touch of hand on shoulder
Bidding grief be gone,
I forget the loneliness of travel
For the while the parted ways are one,—
Know the meaning of the world's great gladness   65
Underneath the sun.
That's the story of my sounding sea-bells,
Chiming all night long,—
The eternal cadence of sea-sorrow   70

For Man's lot and immemorial wrong,—
The lost strain that haunts this human dwelling
With a ghost of song.
Nay, but is there any lost sea-city
Buried in the main,
Where we shall go down in days hereafter,   75
Having said good-bye to grief and pain,
Joy and love at last made one with beauty,
Glad and free again?
You believe not? Hark, there comes the tolling
Of my bells once more,   80
That far-heard and faint fantastic music
From my city by the perilous shore,
Sounding the imperious allegiance
I shall not deplore.

THE LANTERNS OF ST. EULALIE

IN the October afternoon
Orange and purple and maroon,
Goes quiet Autumn, lamp in hand,
About the apple-coloured land,
To light in every apple-tree   5
The Lanterns of St. Eulalie.
They glimmer in the orchard shade
Like fiery opals set in jade,—
Crimson and russet and raw gold,
Yellow and green and scarlet old.   10
And O when I am far away
By foaming reel or azure bay,
In crowded street or hot lagoon,
Or under the strange austral moon,—
When the homesickness comes on me   15
For the great Marshes by the sea,
The running dikes, the brimming tide,
And the dark firs on Fundy side,
In dream once more I shall behold,
Like signal lights, those globes of gold   20

Hung out in every apple-tree—
The Lanterns of St. Eulalie.

HOLIDAY

WHAT is this joy to-day,   5

Hope, reparation, reprieve?
Out of the sweltering city,
Out of the blaring streets
And narrow houses of men,
The seaboard express for the North
Forges, and settles for flight
Into the great blue summer,
The wide, sweet, opulent noon.
Farewell despondency, fear,   10
Ambition, and pitiless greed,
And sordid unlovely regrets!
And thou, frail spirit in me,
My journey-fellow these years,
Behold, thy brothers the elms,   15
And thy sisters the daisies, are here.
Thou, too, shalt grow and be glad,
Companioned of innocence now,
In the long hours of joy.
How will it be that day,   20
When the dark train is ready,
And the inexorable gong
Sounds on the platform of Time.

MARIGOLDS

THE marigolds are nodding;
I wonder what they know.
Go, listen very gently;
You may persuade them so.
Go, be their little brother,   5
As humble as the grass,
And lean upon the hill-wind,
And watch the shadows pass.
Put off the pride of knowledge,
Put by the fear of pain;   10
You may be counted worthy
To live with them again.
Be Darwin in your patience,
Be Chaucer in your love;
They may relent and tell you   15
What they are thinking of.

A PRELUDE

THIS is the sound of the Word   5

From the waters of sleep,
The rain-soft voice that was heard
On the face of the deep,
When the fog was drawn back like a veil, and the sentinel
tides
Were given their thresholds to keep.
The South Wind said, "Come forth,"
And the West Wind said, "Go far!"
And the silvery sea-folk heard,
Where their weed tents are,   10
From the long slow lift of the blue through the Carib keys,
To the thresh on Sable bar.
This is the Word that went by,
Over sun-land and swale,
The long Aprilian cry,   15
Clear, joyous, and hale,
When the summons went forth to the wild shy broods of the
air,
To bid them once more to the trail.
The South Wind said, "Come forth,"
And the West Wind said, "Be swift!"   20
And the fluttering sky-folk heard,
And the warm dark thrift
Of the nomad blood revived, and they gathered for flight,
By column and pair and drift.
This is the sound of the Word   25
From bud-sheath and blade,
When the reeds and the grasses conferred,
And a gold beam was laid
At the taciturn doors of the forest, where tarried the Sun,
For a sign they should not be dismayed.   30

The South Wind said, "Come forth,"
And the West Wind said, "Be glad!"
The abiding wood-folk heard,
In their new green clad,
Sanguine, mist-silver, and rose, while the sap in their veins 35
Welled up as of old all unsad.
This is the Word that flew
Over snow-marsh and glen,
When the frost-bound slumberers knew,
In tree-trunk and den,   40
Their bidding had come, they questioned not whence nor
why,—   45

They reckoned not whither nor when.
The South Wind said, "Come forth,"
And the West Wind said, "Be wise!"
The wintering ground-folk heard,
Put the dark from their eyes,
Put the sloth from sinew and thew, to wander and dare,—
Forever the old surmise!
This is the Word that came
To the spirit of Man,   50
And shook his soul like a flame
In the breath of a fan,
Till it burned as a light in his eyes, as a colour that grew
And prospered under the tan.
The South Wind said, "Come forth,"   55
And the West Wind said, "Be free!"
Then he rose and put on the new garb,
And knew he should be
The master of knowledge and joy, though sprung from the tribes
Of the earth and the air and the sea.   60

THE NORTHERN MUSE

THE Northern Muse looked up
Into the ancient tree,
Where hang the seven olives,
And twine the roses three.
I heard, like the eternal   5
Susurrus of the sea,
Her *Scire quod sciendum*
Da mihi, Domine!

THE TIME AND THE PLACE

"NEVER the time and the place
And the loved one all together!"
Ah, Browning, that does to tell!
But I have an eagle feather
Hid in my waistcoat too.   5

Yes, once in the wild June weather,
In God's own North befell
The joy not time shall undo
Nor the storm of years efface.
Ah, master Browning, you hear?   10

If ever the time and the place
With aught of thy mood concur,
Far off in my golden year,
The solstice of my prime,
Youth done, age not begun,   15
The moment that soul is ripe
For the little touch of rhyme,
Then hearken! If there but stir
One breath of the Spirit of earth
Through me his frail reed-pipe,   20
(As the hermit-thrush
Rehearses the scene when the joy of the world had birth,
So sure, so fine,
Disturbing the hush,)
Your shall hearken, and hear   25
Take rapture and sense and form in one perfect line
A golden lyric of Her!

UNDER THE ROWANS

I SAW a little river
Running beside a wall,
And over it hung scarlet
The berried rowans tall.
Beside it for a moment   5
The summer-time delayed;
And cooler fell the sunlight
Through centuries of shade.
And there was laughing Bronwen
A-wading to the knee.   10
While still the foolish water
Went racing to the sea.
I whistled, "Love, come over!"
She was too wild to fear
The wildness of the forest,   15
The ruin of the year.
And when the stars above us
Hung in the rowans high,
It was the little river
That made our lullaby.   20

Indoors, to-night, and fire-dreams!
And where I wander, far
Within a shining country   25

That needs no calendar,
There is a little river
Running beside a wall,
And over it hang scarlet
The berried rowans tall.

THE GIRL IN THE POSTER

For A Design By Ethel Reed

WITH her head in the golden lilies,
She reads and is never done.
Why her girlish face so still is,
I know not under the sun.
She is the soul of a woman,   5
Knowing whatever befalls;
And I a lonely human,
Dwelling within her walls.
She is the fair immortal
Daughter of truth and art;   10
And I, at her lowly portal,
May fare and be glad and depart.
In a region forever vernal,
She keeps her lilied state,—
My beautiful calm eternal   15
Mysteriarch of fate.
In a volume great and golden,
Would better beseem a sage,
Her downcast look is holden;
But I cannot see the page.   20

Picture, or printed column,
Or records, or cipherings,—
From the drooping lids so solemn
I guess at marvellous things.
Is it a rune she ponders,—
Word from an outer clime,
Where the spirit quests and wanders
Through long sidereal time?
Would she trammel her heart, or cumber
Her mind with our mortal needs?
Do the shadows quake and slumber
On the book wherein she reads?
I know not. I know her being

Is impulse and mood to mine,
Till I voyage, without foreseeing
For a lost horizon line.
For her the spacious morrow;
But the humble day for me,
In the little house of sorrow
By the unbefriending sea.

Her hair is a raven glory;
Her chin is pointed and small;
What is the wonderful story
Keeps her forever in thrall?
Her mouth is little and childly;
Her brow is innocent broad;
Meekly she reads and mildly,—
Would neither condemn nor applaud.
Would that I too, a-reading,
Might half of her wisdom find,
In the gold flowers there unheeding,—
The calm of an open mind!
Day long, as I keep the homely
Round of my chambers here,
Her beauty is modest and comely,
Her presence living and near.
Till it seems I must recover
A day in the ilex grove,
Where I was a destined lover,
And she was destined for love.

I remember the woods we strayed in,
And the mountain paths we trod,
When she was a Doric maiden,
And I was a young Greek god.
And I have the haunting fancy,
The moment my back is turned,
By some Eastern necromancy
Only the artists have learned,
Two great grave eyes are lifted
To follow me round the room,
And a sudden breath has shifted
A leaf in the Book of Doom.

ON THE STAIRS

FROM glory up to glory
On the great stairs of time,
I track the ghostly whisper
That bids a mortal climb.
I pass the gorgeous threshold   5
Of many an open door,
Where, luring and illusive,
The pageant gleams once more.
Up the Potomac Valley
I see the April come;   10
Here it is May in Paris;
Here is my Ardise home;
These are the Scituate marshes;
This is a Norman town;
These are the dikes of Grand Pré;—   15
Ah, tell no more, Renown!
I pass the open portals,
Irresolute and fond,—
Desert the masque of beauty
For Beauty's self beyond.   20

For down the echoing stairway
Of being, I have heard
The faint immortal secret
Shut in a mortal word,—
The tawny velvet accent   25
Of Lilith, as she came
Into the great blue garden
And breathed her lover's name.

THE DESERTED INN

I CAME to a deserted inn,
Standing apart, alone;
A place where human joy had been,
And only winds made moan.
I entered by the spacious hall,   5
With not a soul to see;
The echo of my own footfall
Was ghostly there to me.
I came upon a sudden door,
Which gave me no reply;   10
The more I questioned it, the more
A questioner was I.   15

I lingered by the mouldy stair,
And by the dusty sill;
And when my faint heart said, "Beware!"
The silence said, "Be still!"
From room to room I caught the stir
Of garments vanishing,—
The stillness trying to demur,
When one has ceased to sing.   20

Like shadows of the clouds which make
The loneliness of noon,
The thing I could not overtake
Was but an instant gone.
'T was summer when I reached the inn;   25
The apples were in bloom;
Before I left, the snow drove in,
The frost was like a doom.
At last I came upon the book
Where visitors of yore   30
Had writ their names, ere joy forsook
The House of Rest-no-more.
Poor fellow-travellers, beset
With hungers not of earth!
Did you, too, tarry here in debt   35
For things of perished worth?
Did something lure you like a strain
Of music wild and vast,
Only to freeze your blood again
With jeers when you had passed?   40

Did visions of a fairer thing
Than God has ever made
Fleet through your doorways in the spring,
And would not be delayed?
Did beauty in a half-made song,   45
A smile of mystery,
Departing, leave you here to long
For what could never be,—
And thenceforth you were friends of peace,
Acquainted with unrest,   50
Whom no perfection could release
From the unworldly quest?
I heard a sound of women's tears,
More desolate than the sea,   55

Sigh through the chambers of the years
Unto eternity.
And then beyond the fathom of sense
I knew, as the dead know,
My lost ideal had journeyed thence
Unnumbered years ago.   60

And from that dwelling of the night,
With the gray dusk astir,
I waited for the first gold light
To let me forth to Her.

THE OPEN DOOR

LOVE me, love me not,—
What is that to me?
I have not forgot
When we two were three.
She who loved us twain   5
Well enough to die,—
Can we love again
While her ghost stands by?
Love me, love me not,—
I can love no more,   10
For the empty cot
And the open door.

JAPANESE LOVE SONG

HOW you start away!
—As a flame starts from a gust.
Flame-heart o' the dust!
Sudden startle of dismay!
Swift triumph in distrust!   5

Flash and tremble of escape,
Fierce with desire!
Rippled water shot with fire
Wary of the rape
Of the eyes that sire!   10

Radiant no-and-yes!
Deer-flight and panther-thirst!
Blest and accurst!
Sword-splendour past the guess   15

Of Heaven's best and Hell's worst!

So you sprang up from yourself,
Burnt to supremacies,
Star-demoned by a kiss—
Night turned fire-elf,—
Wonder and all amiss!   20

"HOW SHOULD LOVE KNOW?"

HOW should Love know
The face of sorrow?
Love is so young a thing!
Roses that blow
To-day, lie to-morrow   5
Faded and withering.

UNFORESEEN

WHY did I kiss you, sweet?
Nor you nor I can say.
You might have said some commonplace,
I might have turned away.
No thought was in our hearts   5
Of what we were to be.
Fate sent a madness on our souls
And swept us out to sea.
Fate, between breath and breath,
Has made the world anew,   10
And the bare skies of yesterday
Are all aflame with you.

CHILD'S SONG

But just across the furthest hill
I know the fairies live.

PLEASE, sir, take me in your carriage
And ride me home! You see,
I've been to find the fairies
And I'm tired as I can be.
I crossed the meadow and the brook   5

And climbed Rapalye's hill,
But when I reached the top of it
There was another still.

HARMONICS

"TRUTH is not a creed,
For it does not need
Ever an apology.
Truth is not an ology;
'T is not part, but all.   5
Priests and savans shall
Never solve the mystic
Problem. The artistic
Mind alone of all can tell
What is Truth.   10

"Poet, thou art wisest;
Dogmas thou despisest—
Science little prizest.
Tell us, for thou knowest well,
What is Truth."   15

Spake the seekers to an holy
Bard, who answered, mild and lowly—
This, all this, was in the olden
Days when Saturn's reign was golden —

"Shall I read the riddle—   20
Tell you what is Truth?
Truth is not the first
Not the last or middle;
'T is the beautiful
And symmetric whole,   25
Embracing best and worst,
Embracing age and youth.
"All the universe
Is one mighty song,
Wherein every star   30
Chants out loud and strong
Each set note and word
It must aye rehearse.
Though the parts may jar,
The whole is as one chord."   35

ORNITHOLOGY

SWEETHEART, do you see up yonder through the leaves
The elm tree interweaves,
How that cock-sparrow chases his brown mate?
Look, where she perches now
Upon the bough   5
And turns her head to see if he pursue her,
Half frightened, half elate
To have so bold and beautiful a wooer.
See, he alights beside her. How his wings
Quiver with amorous passionings!   10
How voluble their chattering courtship is!
Soon will he know
Love's joys in overflow,
Love's extreme ecstasies.

No, off she flies!   15
Just as she seemed about to be subdued
To his impetuous desire!
How angrily he scolds, with wicked eyes
Following her flight, and turns his tiny ire
Against the innocent tree and pecks the wood!   20
While she—ah, the coquette!—
Lurks yonder in the cleft where the great tree
Breaks into boughs, and peeps about to see
If he is coming yet.
She's in for a game of lovers' hide-and-seek,   25
And longs to have him find the hiding-place,
Although she feigns concealment, so to pique
His passion to a chase.
In vain—he will not look
For all her sweet allurements. Out she whisks   30
Demurely from her nook,
As if she did not see and were not seen,
And perks herself and frisks
Her delicate tail as a lady flirts her fan,
And now slips back again to her retreat   35
And waits for one hushed moment in serene
Unfluttered expectation that the plan
Have issue sweet.
What, will he not come yet?
See how she glances at him unawares,   40
Tosses her head and gives herself high airs
In such a pretty pet.   45

Cruel! he turns away,
Affecting unconcern.
All those endearing wiles are wrought in vain.
Alas, unlucky flirt! too late you learn
That long delays will make the eagerest lover
Aweary of pursuing. Nay,
Too late you fly half way to him again.
You will not so recover   50
The passion that you played with. Off he flies
And now is lost in the thick shade
Of lilac bushes further down the glade.
Another mistress charms his amorous eyes.
Have a care, sweetheart, or as he some day   55

I too will fly away.

TO AN IRIS

THOU art a golden iris
Under a purple wall,
Whereon the burning sunlight
And greening shadows fall.
What Summer night's enchantment   5
Took up the garden mould,
And with the falling star-dust
Refined it to such gold?
What wonder of white magic
Bidding thy soul aspire,   10
Filled that luxurious body
With languor and with fire?
Wert thou not once a beauty
In Persia or Japan,
For whom, by toiling seaway   15
Or dusty caravan,
Of old some lordly lover
Brought countless treasure home
Of gems and silk and attar,
To pleasure thee therefrom?   20

Pale amber from the Baltic,
Soft rugs of Indian ply,
Stuffs from the looms of Bagdad
Stained with the Tyrian dye.
Were thy hands bright with henna,   25
Thy lashes black with kohl,   30

Thy voice like silver water
Out of an earthen bowl?
Or was thy only tent-cloth
The blue Astartean night,
Thy soul to beauty given,
Thy body to delight?
Wert thou not well desired,
And was not life a boon,
When Tanis held in Sidon   35
Her Mysteries of the Moon?
There in her groves of ilex
The nightingales made ring
With the mad lyric chorus
Of youth and love and Spring,   40

Were thou not glad to worship
With some blond Paphian boy,
Illumined by new knowledge
And intimate with joy?
And did not the Allmother   45
Smile in the hushed dim light,
Hearing thy stifled laughter
Disturb her holy rite?
Ah, well thou must have served her
In wise and gracious ways,   50
With more than vestal fervour,
A loved one all thy days!
And dost thou, then, revisit
Our borders at her will,
Child of the sultry rapture,   55
Waif of the Orient still?
Because thy love was fearless
And fond and strong and free,
Art thou not her last witness
To our apostasy?   60

Just at the height of summer,
The joy-days of the year,
She bids, for our reproval,
Thy radiance appear.
Oh, Iris, let thy spirit   65
Enkindle our gross clay,
Bring back the lost earth-passion
For beauty to our day!   70

To-night, when down the marshes
The lilac half-lights fade,
And on the rosy shore-line
No earthly spell is laid,
I would be thy new lover,
With the dark life renewed
By our great mother Tanis   75
And thy solicitude.
Feel slowly change this vesture
Of mortal flesh and bone,
Transformed by her soft witch-work
To one more like thine own.   80

Become but as the rain-wind
(Who am but dust indeed),
To slake thy velvet ardour
And soothe thy darling need.
To dream and waken with thee   85
Under the night's blue sail,
As the wild odours freshen,
Till the white stars grow pale.

BERRIS YARE

A LEGEND OF THE
BRIER ROSE
Once in the fairy tale
sweet Rose Brier
Climbed to the bent of
her heart's desire.
Poor Rose Brier, as I've
heard tell,
Never came back with
her folk to dwell.
This is the legend of
sweet Brier Rose
Out of a country that
nobody knows.
Dear Brier Rose could
never aspire,
Yet came at length to
her heart's desire.

SINGLE-HEART Brier Rose, gipsy desire   5

Eyes of the Hush-hound and crispy dark hair,
Lyric of summer dawn, dew-drench and fire,
Wilding and gentle and shy Berris Yare!
Bide with me, Brier Rose, here for an hour.

See the red sun, like a great royal rose,
Flung down the gray for the winter's king flower,
While Marden sleeps in his mantle of snows.
Far-wandered Brier Rose, how came we here,
Alien, ease-loving, alone in this North?   10

White winter, laid at the heart of the year,
Heeds us not, needs us not, leads us not forth.
Long ago, Brier Rose, loved we not thus?
Was it when Alaric marched against Rome?
Others might win the world; leave love for us!   15

Dost thou remember the Visigoth home?
Think again, Summer-heart. Canst not recall
When thou wert Brier Rose gladsome and fair?
How I remember thee, shapely and tall,—
Far away, long ago thee, Berris Yare!   20

Sword-play for Brier Rose, war song and march;
Throstle for joy bade the waking world sing;
Morning waved banners out bold from the larch;
When we went down on the legions in spring.
Bracelets for Brier Rose, wrought Roman gold;   25

Tribute and trophy poured plenty as sand;
Frost on the flower-garth, rime on the wold;
When we came triumphing back through the land.
How thy cheek, Brier Rose, signalled aflame;
How the song rang of the foemen downborne;   30

How brown eyes kindled up as we came
Through the bowed ranks of the gleaming red corn!
Then the long days when the harvest was done;
Hand in hand, hill and dale, thou and I there,
Dreaming of far-off new isles of the sun,—   35

Never a dream of this day, Berris Yare!
Fairy-tale, home-royal red of the rose,
Wilding and well-a-day sweet of the brier!
Here in the gray world engirdled with snows,
Watch the slow sun set the hill tops afire!   40

What if, my Brier Rose, love were just this:
One gracious core of the whirled starry dust,
Round which the swinging motes, never amiss,   45

Traverse the infinite dark as they must.
All the earth else a mere seed-plot of clay,
Fruitless and flowerless, mixed garden mould,
Awaiting the gardener, inert, to obey
When the first sunbeam bids, "Blossoms, unfold!"
Then the whole host of them, gold daffodils;
Poppies so well of red dreamland aware;   50
Michaelmas daisies smoke blue on the hills;
None like my Brier Rose, my Berris Yare.
Acres of apple-bloom, maids at the door;
Wind-hands of summer with heart-strings to pull;
Fruit to the harvesting, men to the war;   55
Come winter speedily, love's year is full.
Cherry-mouth Brier Rose, washed in the dew,
Kiss me again before daylight be done,—
Once for the old love and twice for the new,
Thrice for the dearest love under the sun!   60

Gold heart of sundowns and summers forgot!
Treasure of solitude, simple and wild!
God in our poem missed rhyme by a jot;
Life never yet with poor love reconciled.
Wert thou not Brier Rose once on a time?   65
Attar of memory, chivalry's dare!
Love's the lost echo of flute-notes at prime,
Wondrous, far wandering. Hark, Berris Yare!
Only the leaves of the oaks brown and sere,
Garrulous wiseacre, doting old leaves,   70
Go whisper others your cumber-world fear,—
Kill-joy foreboding that croaks and deceives!
Heed them not, Brier Rose. Hearken again!
Nothing? No breath of the music to be?
Ah! but I hear the low footfall of rain,—   75
April's clan Joy making in from the sea.
April. Think, Brier Rose! how the earth's heart,
Brook rapture, bird rapture, riot of rills,
Stirs with old dreams that rend slumber apart!
Then the long twilight dim-blue on the hills.   80

Hills that will talk to me when thou art gone,—
That old solicitude, calming despair,
Sweet as the sundown, austere as the dawn,—
"Love that lost Brier Rose, found Berris Yare."
April. Then, Brier Rose, some silent eve,   85

While the dusk hears the hill-rivers give tongue,
In the first swamp-robin I shall perceive
One golden strain that, when being was young,
Kin to the world-cry and kith to the stars,
Pierced human sorrows such ages ago.   90
Leisurely fluting in gold, broken bars
Comes the rehearsal, serenely and slow,
Prelude, re-prelude; and then the full throat,
Mellowly, mellowly —stops mid-stream—
Wearily, wearily.—What may denote   95
Such incompleteness? Can love be the theme?
Brother of Brier Rose, flute-master mine
(Then will this heart-ache out cry to him there),
Thou with the secret in that flute of thine,
Where is my dream-fellow, lost Berris Yare?   100

A MODERN ECLOGUE

SHE

IF you were ferryman at Charon's ford,
And I came down the bank and called to you,
Waved you my hand and asked to come aboard,
And threw you kisses there, what would you do?
Would there be such a crowd of other girls,   5
Pleading and pale and lonely as the sea,
You'd growl in your old beard, and shake your curls,
And say there was no room for little me?
Would you remember each of them in turn?
Put all your faded fancies in the bow,   10
And all the rest before you in the stern,
And row them out with panic on your brow?
If I came down and offered you my fare
And more beside, could you refuse me there?

HE

IF I were ferryman in Charon's place,   15
And ran that crazy scow with perilous skill,
I should be so worn out with keeping trace
Of gibbering ghosts and bidding them sit still,
If you should come with daisies in your hands,
Strewing their petals on the sombre stream,—   20
"He will come," and "He won't come," down the lands
Of pallid reverie and ghostly dream,—
I would let every clamouring shape stand there,   25

And give its shadowy lungs free vent in vain,
While you with earthly roses in your hair,
And I grown young at sight of you again,
Went down the stream once more at half-past seven
To find some brand-new continent of heaven.

FROM THE CLIFF

HERE on this ledge, the broad plain stretched below,
The calm hills smiling in immortal mirth,
The blue sky whitening as it nears the earth,
Afar where all the summits are aglow,
I feel a mighty wind upon me blow   5
Like God's breath kindling in my soul a birth
Of turbulent music struggling to break girth.
I pass with Dante through eternal woe,
Quiver with Sappho's passion at my heart,
See Pindar's chariots flashing past the goal,   10
Triumph o'er splendours of unutterable light
And know supremely this, O God,—Thou art,
Feeling in all this tumult of my soul
Grand kinship with the glory of Thy might.

SEA SONNETS

OUT with the tide—afar, afar, afar,
Where will the wide dark take us, you and me—
The darkness and the tempest and the sea?
How long we waited where the tall ships are,
Disconsolate and safe within the bar!   5
Ocean forever calling us, but we—
God, how we stifled there, nor dared be free
With a sharp knife and night and the wild dare!
But now, the hawser cut, adrift, away—
Mad with escape, what care we to what doom   10
The bitter night may bear us? Lost, alone,
In a vague world of roaring surge astray,
Out with the tide and into the unknown,
Compassed about with rapture and the gloom!

II

We two, waifs, wide-eyed and without fear,   15
With the dark swirl of life about our prow,
The hollow, heedless swash of year on year
That bears us on and recks not where nor how!   20

Our skiff is but a feather on the foam,
No mighty galleon strong to meet the storm—
An open boat—God's gift to us for home,
And but each other's arms to keep us warm!
What port for us to make? Our only star
To steer by is the star of missing sails,
Our only haven where the kelpies are— 25
Yet, you great merchantment with freighted bales,
Rebel and lost and aimless as we go,
We keep a joy your pride can never know.

III

Moon of my midlight! Moon of the dark sea,
Where like a petrel's ghost my sloop is driven! 30
Behold, about me and under and over me,
The darkness and the waters and the heaven—
Huge, shapeless monsters as of worlds in birth,
Dragons of Fate, that hold me not in scope—
Bar up my way with fierce, indifferent mirth, 35
And fall in giant frolic on my hope.
Their next mad rush may whelm me in the wave,
The dreaded horror of the sightless deep—
Only thy love, like moonlight, pours to save
My soul from the despairs that lunge and leap. 40
Moon of my night, though hell and death assail,
The tremble of thy light is on my sail.

AT A SUMMER RESORT

I MISS you so by day, your look, your walk,
The rustle of your draperies on the stair,
Our Leyden-jar-fuls of electric talk,
The sense of you about me everywhere.
The people bore me in the boarding-house, 5
I hardly can accord them yes or no;
The beauty of the valleys can arouse
No such elation as a year ago.
But when the last dull guest has gone to bed
And only crickets keep me company, 10
In the mesmeric night when truth is said—
When you, dear loveliness with drooping eye,
Demurely enter through the unreal wall,
And I forget you went away at all.

NEW YORK

THE low line of the walls that lie outspread
Miles on long miles, the fog and smoke and slime,
The wharves and ships with flags of every clime,
The domes and steeples rising overhead!
It is not these. Rather it is the tread   5
Of the million heavy feet that keep sad time
To heavy thoughts, the want that mothers crime,
The weary toiling for a bitter bead,
The perishing of poets for renown,
The shriek of shame from the concealing waves.   10
Ah, me! how many heart-beats day by day
Go to make up the life of the vast town!
O myriad dead in unremembered graves!
O torrent of the living down Broadway!

A GROTESQUE

OUR Gothic minds have gargoyle fancies.
Odd,
That there will come a day when you and I
Shall not be you and I, that we shall lie,
We two, in the damp earth-mould, above each clod   5
A drunken headstone in the neglected sod,
Thereon the phrase, Hic Jacet, worn awry,
And then our virtues, bah!—and piety—
Perhaps some cheeky reference to God!
And haply after many a century   10
Some spectacled old man shall drive the birds
A moment from their song in the lonely spot
And make a copy of the quaint old words—
They will then be quaint and old—and all for what?
To fill a gap in a genealogy.   15

WHEN THE PRIEST LEFT

WHAT did he say?
To seek love otherwhere
Nor bind the soul to clay?
It may be so—I cannot tell—
But I know that life is fair,   5
And love's bold clarion in the air
Outdins his little vesper-bell.
Love God? Can I touch God with both my hands?
Can I breathe in his hair and brush his cheek   10

He is too far to seek.
If nowhere else be love, who understands
What thing it is?
This love is but a name that wise men speak.
God hath no lips to kiss.
Let God be; surely, if he will,   15
At the end of days,
He can win love as well as praise.
Why must we spill
The human love out at his feet?
Let be this talk of good and ill!   20
Though God be God, art thou not fair and sweet?
Open the window; let the air
Blow in on us.
It is enough to find you fair,
To touch with fingers timorous   25
Your sunlit hair,—
To turn my body to a prayer,
And kiss you—thus.

THE GIFT OF ART

I DREAMED that child was born; and at his birth
The Angel of the Word stood by the hearth
And spake to her that bare him: "Look without!
Behold the beauty of the Day, the shout
Of colour to glad colour, rocks and trees   5
And sun and sea and wind and sky! All these
Are God's expression, art-work of his hand,
Which men must love ere they may understand,
By which alone he speaks till they have grace
To hear his voice and look upon his face.   10
For first and last of all things in the heart
Of God as man the glory is of art.
What gift could God bestow or man beseech,
Save spirit unto spirit uttered speech?
Wisdom were not, for God himself could find   15
No way to reach the unresponsive mind,
Sweet Love were dead, and all the crowded skies
A loneliness and not a Paradise.
Teach the child language, mother. . . ."

TO JAMES WHITCOMB RILEY

THOUGH aiblins some deserve as highly   5

O' that braw winsome lass an' wily
Wha gi'es a kiss to bardies slyly
An' sets 'em liltin',
I ken there's nane can equal Riley
To 'scape her jiltin'.
How comes it, man, ye ken sae well
The Muse's tricks? Hae ye a spell
To keep her sae a' to yoursel',
An' fu' in Fame's e'e?   10
Fame?—let *that* hizzie gae to hell!
Here's to you, Jamesie!

TO RUDYARD KIPLING

WHAT need have you of praising? Could I find
Some lonely poet no one praises yet,
Him rather would I choose, that he might know
A fellow-craftsman knew him, marked him, loved.
But you—the whole world praises you. What need   5
Have you of any speech I have to give?
Yet for the craft's sake I must give you praise;
And for the craft's sake you will pardon me.
But I would rather meet you face to face
And talk of other and indifferent things,   10
And say no word of all that I would say,
Praise and thanksgiving for your splendid song,
Praise and the pride of the empires of the Blood—
But leave you, silent, as we English do—
And you would know —and you would understand.   15

ROMANY SIGNS

On the publication of "Patrins," by Louise Imogen Guiney.

IF I should wander out some afternoon
About the end of May or early June,
And at a crossroads in the hills discover
A spray of apple or a sprig of clover,
Set for a sign to tell who went that way,   5
Which road he took and how he fared that day,
"Ho, ho," I'd whistle, "here's a gipsy token,
As plain as if the very word were spoken."   10

Then down I turn, hot foot, and off I trudge
Hard on his trail, while sceptics mutter, "Fudge!"
They know the way, these travel-wise Egyptians,
And I—enough to follow their inscriptions.
So, bless you! in a mile or two at most,
I've overtaken, almost passed, my host
Camped in the finest grove in all the county   15
And bidding me to supper on his bounty.
There's nothing like a bit of open sky
To give a touch of poetry to pie;
And here's a poem (call it Sphinx in Myrtle)
Would make an alderman forget his turtle.   20

Now, there's a Romany in Auburndale,
Wild as a faun and sound as cakes and ale,
One of the tribe of Stevenson and Borrow,
Who live to-day and let alone to-morrow.
(God keeps a few still living in the sun,—   25
The man who wrote The Seven Seas, for one,
And Island Stoddard,—just to prove the folly
Of smug repose and pious melancholy.)
So when I see her signal in the hedge,
(I mean her new book on the counter's edge,)   30
"Ho, ho," say I, "that Guiney's broken loose again,
Cut a new quill and put her craft to use again."
Enough for me! I'm off. And, fellows all,
Who could resist the Auburndalean call
To go a-foraging? That's what the spring's for,   35
What bards have wits and bumblebees have wings for.
I'll warrant here's a road to Arcady
With goodly cheer and merry company,
Skirting the pleasant foot-hills of Philosophy,
Far from the quaggy marshes of Theosophy.   40

O for the trail, wherever it may lead,
From small credulity to larger creed,
Till we behold this world without detraction
As God did seven times with satisfaction!

THE MAN WITH THE TORTOISE

TO W.M.F.

SUCH curious things the mind bids stay,   5

Of the thousand and one that pass it by!
The morning we walked through Paris in May,
If you remember as well as I,
There happened—a nothing—an incident—
One of those trifles that flit half seen,
Save where the spirit sits intent,
Furtive and shy at her window screen.
The servants' gossip of eye and ear
May surge and hum at her door in spring   10
Of the pageant of beauty drawing near,
But she—she is watching a stranger thing!
The myriad rabble of fact and form
May gleam till the senses dance with glee;
But calm, unmoved as the very norm   15
And centre of being, muses she;
Indifferent to loveliness, line or hue,
Till a chance bird-wing or a slant sun-ray
May fall as prompt as an actor's cue,
And there is her part. So it was that day.   20

We had turned from your door in the rue Vignon,
The third on the left from the Madelaine. . . .
Forget it? There's no forgetting when one
Is come at length to his Castle in Spain.
For you were the friend I had loved of old,   25
And pictured so often in Paris here,
And promised myself some day to hold
Unaltered and safe and sound, no fear.
For our mistress Nature is great and wise,
And the love of her is eternity;   30
But there comes a day when a man must rise
And go where the heart in him longs to be.
So the sea was crossed, and the hour was come;
It was hand on shoulder with us once more.
There was speech enough though the lips were dumb,   35
When I stood at last at your modest door.
Your breakfast of capon and Burgundy,
Our talk of Harvard and Norton's fame,
And your friend the Druse, with cigars laid by—
Your gift from the Baroness What's-her-name.   40

Then into the street of the Capucines
In the blaze of the Paris sun we strolled;
Once more at touch of your blithe light mien   45

I knew how a springflower breaks the mould.
Through the gay May weather when life was good,
Idly we sauntered from block to block,
Till round a corner appeared, and stood,
A fellow in workman's cap and smock,
Basket on arm and whistling low
To something held in the rough right hand.   50

A tortoise! Yes, and the creature, so,
Grown tame at the music's soft command.
Emboldened to peep from the safe snug shell,
Had pushed up its head to the whistler's face,
The least of wild things under the spell   55

Of the last and humblest of Orpheus' race.
A fragment from some Greek Idyllist,
The plain good look of the bolder text,
Preserving for us the colour and gist
Of a simple age and a life unvexed.   60

Did the beast recall how the syrinx blew
When his father Pan first notched a reed?
Was it some familiar note he knew
In the workman's whistle that made him heed?
Did there wake remembrance dim and large   65

Of the drench and glamour, the mist and gleam,
Of a morning once by the shining marge
And murmurous run of a Dorian stream?
Or was it only the reedy plash
Of a Norman river, sunny and small,   70

Where a sound of wind in the scarlet ash,
Blown high, blown low, once held him thrall?
Was there nought but the sweet luxurious thrill
Of the senses, strung to rhythm and time?
No shadow of soul, to remember and fill   75

The shell that day with a joy sublime?
So still, as for very life he feared
To lose one note of the wild sweet strain.
Ah, mortal, blow till thy breath has cleared
Ages of dust from a haunted brain!   80

And often I think, as the days go by,
Of our whistling man and the small mute friend
He had charmed. And a scrap of legendry
Has always given the thought a trend.
An Indian myth (you will pardon its worth!)   85

Says a tortoise, firm in his arching shell,
Upbears the creature that bears the earth;
But what holds the tortoise none can tell.
The tortoise, I venture, may symbolise
The husk of being, the outward world,   90
The substance of beauty, each form and guise
Where the lurking mind is ensheathed, encurled.
And suppose at the lip of the shell there stood
A mortal bent on the strange and new,
Trying each cadence wild and rude,   95
Till the magic melody he blew!
What glimpse to that cunning dweller in clay
Might not the old tortoise Earth afford
Of her very self, some morning in May,
Emerged for once to the perfect chord!   100

THE SCEPTICS

IT was the little leaves beside the road.
Said Grass, "What is that sound
So dismally profound,
That detonates and desolates the air?"   5
"That is St. Peter's bell,"
Said rain-wise Pimpernel;
"He is music to the godly,
Though to us he sounds so oddly,
And he terrifies the faithful unto prayer."   10

Then something very like a groan
Escaped the naughty little leaves.
Said Grass, "And whither track
These creatures all in black,
So woebegone and penitent and meek?"   15
"They're mortals bound for church,"
Said the little Silver Birch;
"They hope to get to heaven
And have their sins forgiven,
If they talk to God about it once a week."   20

And something very like a smile
Ran through the naughty little leaves.
Said Grass, "What is that noise
That startles and destroys
Our blessed summer brooding when we're tired?"   25

"That's folk a-praising God,"
Said the tough old cynic Clod;
"They do it every Sunday,
They'll be all right on Monday;
It's just a little habit they've acquired."   30

And laughter spread among the little leaves.

A THANKSGIVING

I THANK thee, Earth, for water good,
The sea's great bath of buoyant green
Or the cold mountain torrent's flood,
That I may keep this body clean.
I thank thee more for goodly wine,   5
That wise as Omar I may be,
Or Horace when he went to dine
With Lydia or with Lalage.

A STACCATO TO O LE LUPE

O LE LUPE, Gelett Burgess, this is very sad to find:
In The Bookman for September, in a manner most unkind,
There appears a half-page picture, makes me think I've lost
my mind.
They have reproduced a window,—Doxey's window,—(I
dare say
In your rambles you have seen it, passed it twenty times a
day,)   5
As "A Novel Exhibition of Examples of Decay."
There is Nordau we all sneer at, and Verlaine we all adore,
And a little book of verses with its betters by the score,
With three faces on the cover I believe I've seen before.
Well, here's matter for reflection, makes me wonder where I
am.   10
Here is Ibsen the gray lion, linked to Beardsley the black
lamb.
I was never out of Boston; all that I can say is, "Damn!"
Who could think, in two short summers we should cause so
much remark,
With no purpose but our pastime, and to make the public
hark,
When I soloed on The Chap-Book, and you answered with
The Lark!   15
     20

Do young people take much pleasure when they read that
sort of thing?
"Well, they buy it," answered Doxey, "and I take what it will
bring.
Publishers may dread extinction—not with such fads on the
string.
"There is always sale for something, and demand for what is
new.
These young men who are so restless, and have nothing
else to do,
Like to think there is 'a movement,' just to keep themselves
in view.
"There is nothing in Decadence but the magic of a name.
People talk and papers drivel, scent a vice, and hint a
shame;
And all that is good for business, helps to boom my little
game."
But when I sit down to reason, think to stand upon my
nerve,   25
Meditate on portly leisure with a balance in reserve,
In he comes with his "Decadence!" like a fly in my preserve.
I can see myself, O Burgess, half a century from now,
Laid to rest among the ghostly, like a broken toy somehow,
All my lovely songs and ballads vanished with your "Purple
Cow."   30

But I will return some morning, though I know it will be hard,
To Cornhill among the bookstalls, and surprise some minor
bard,
Turning over their old rubbish for the treasures we discard.
I shall warn him like a critic, creeping when his back is
turned,
"Ink and paper, dead and done with; Doxey spent what
Doxey earned;   35
Poems doubtless are immortal, where a poem can be
discerned!"
How his face will go to ashes, when he feels his empty
purse!
How he'll wish his vogue were greater; plume himself it is no
worse;
Then go bother the dear public with his puny little verse!
Don't I know how he will pose it; patronize our larger time;   40
"Poor old Browning; little Kipling; what attempts they made
to rhyme!"   45

Just let me have half an hour with that nincompoop sublime!
I will haunt him like a purpose, I will ghost him like a fear;
When he least expects my presence, I'll be mumbling in his ear,
"O Le Lupe lived in Frisco, and I lived in Boston here.

"Never heard of us? Good heavens, can you never have been told
Of the Larks we used to publish, and the Chap-Books that we sold?
Where are all our first editions?" I feel damp and full of mould.

A SPRING FEELING

I THINK it must be spring. I feel
All broken up and thawed.
I'm sick of everybody's "wheel;"
I'm sick of being jawed.
I am too winter-killed to live,   5

Cold-sour through and through.
O Heavenly Barber, come and give
My soul a dry shampoo!
I'm sick of all these nincompoops,
Who weep through yards of verse,   10

And all these sonneteering dupes
Who whine and froth and curse.
I'm sick of seeing my own name
Tagged to some paltry line,
While this old corpus without shame   15

Sits down to meat and wine.
I'm sick of all these Yellow Books,
And all these Bodley Heads;
I'm sick of all these freaks and spooks
And frights in double leads.   20

When good Napoleon's publisher
Was dangled from a limb,
He should have had an editor
On either side of him.
I'm sick of all this taking on   25

Under a foreign name;
For when you call it decadent,
It's rotten just the same.
I'm sick of all this puling trash   30

And namby-pamby rot,—
A Pegasus you have to thrash
To make him even trot!
An Age-end Art! I would not give,
For all their plotless plays,
One round Falstaffian adjective   35
Or one Miltonic phrase.
I'm sick of all this poppycock
In bilious green and blue;
I'm tired to death of taking stock
Of everything that's "New."   40

New Art, New Movements, and New Schools,
All maimed and blind and halt!
And all the fads of the New Fools
Who cannot earn their salt.
I'm sick of the New Woman, too.   45
Good Lord, she's worst of all.
Her rights, her sphere, her point of view,
And all that folderol!
She makes me wish I were the snake
Inside of Eden's wall,   50
To give the tree another shake,
And see another fall.
I'm very much of Byron's mind;
I like sufficiency;
But just the common garden kind   55
Is good enough for me.
I want to find a warm beech wood,
And lie down, and keep still;
And swear a little; and feel good;
Then loaf on up the hill,   60

And let the Spring house-clean my brain,
Where all this stuff is crammed;
And let my heart grow sweet again;
And let the Age be damned.

HER VALENTINE

WHAT, send her a valentine? Never!
I see you don't know who "she" is.
I should ruin my chances forever;
My hopes would collapse with a fizz.   5

I can't see why she scents such disaster
When I take heart to venture a word;
I've no dream of becoming her master,
I've no notion of being her lord.
All I want is to just be her lover!
She's the most up-to-date of her sex,   10
And there's such a multitude of her,
No wonder they call her complex.
She's a bachelor, even when married,
She's a vagabond, even when housed;
And if ever her citadel's carried   15
Her suspicions must not be aroused.
She's erratic, impulsive and human,
And she blunders,—as goddesses can;
But if she's what they call the New Woman,
Then I'd like to be the New Man.   20

I'm glad she makes books and paints pictures,
And typewrites and hoes her own row,
And it's quite beyond reach of conjectures
How much further she's going to go.
When she scorns, in the L-road, my proffer   25
Of a seat and hangs on to a strap;
I admire her so much, I could offer
To let her ride up on my lap.
Let her undo the stays of the ages,
That have cramped and confined her so long!   30
Let her burst through the frail candy cages
That fooled her to think they were strong!
She may enter life's wide vagabondage,
She may do without flutter or frill,
She may take off the chains of her bondage,—   35
And anything else that she will.
She may take me off, for example,
And she probably does when I'm gone.
I'm aware the occasion is ample;
That's why I so often take on.   40

I'm so glad she can win her own dollars
And know all the freedom it brings.
I love her in shirt-waists and collars,
I love her in dress-reform things.
I love her in bicycle skirtlings—   45
Especially when there's a breeze—   50

I love her in crinklings and quirklings
And anything else that you please.
I dote on her even in bloomers—
If Parisian enough in their style—
In fact, she may choose her costumers,
Wherever her fancy beguile.
She may box, she may shoot, she may wrestle,
She may argue, hold office or vote,
She may engineer turret or trestle,   55
And build a few ships that will float.
She may lecture (all lectures but curtain)
Make money, and naturally spend,
If I let her have her way, I'm certain
She'll let me have mine in the end!   60

IN PHILISTIA

OF all the places on the map,
Some queer and others queerer,
Arcadia is dear to me,
Philistia is dearer.
There dwell the few who never knew   5
The pangs of heavenly hunger,
As fresh and fair and fond and frail
As when the world was younger.
If there is any sweeter sound
Than bobolinks or thrushes,   10
It is the frou-frou of their silks—
The roll of their barouches.
I love them even when they're good,
As well as when they're sinners—
When they are sad and worldly wise   15
And when they are beginners.
(I say I do; of course the fact,
For better or for worse, is,
My unerratic life denies
My too erotic verses.)   20

I dote upon their waywardness,
Their foibles and their follies.
If there's a madder pate than Di's,
Perhaps it may be Dolly's.
They have no "problems" to discuss,   25
No "theories" to discover;   30

They are not "new"; and I—I am
Their very grateful lover.
I care not if their minds confuse
Alastor with Aladdin;
And Cimabue is far less
To them than Chimmie Fadden.
They never heard of William Blake,
Nor saw a Botticelli;
Yet one is, "Yours till death, Louise," 35
And one, "Your loving Nelly."
They never tease me for my views,
Nor tax me with my grammar;
Nor test me on the latest news,
Until I have to stammer. 40

They never talk about their "moods,"
They never know they have them;
The world is good enough for them,
And that is why I love them.
They never puzzle me with Greek, 45
Nor drive me mad with Ibsen;
Yet over forms as fair as Eve's
They wear the gowns of Gibson.

PEACE

THERE is peace, you say. I believe you.
Peace? Ay, we know it well—
Not the peace of the smile of God, but the peace of the leer
of Hell,
Peace, that the rich may fatten and barter their souls for
gain,
Peace, that the hungry may slay and rob the corpse of the
slain, 5
Peace, that the heart of the people may rot with a vile
gangrene.
What though the men are bloodless! What's a man to a
machine?
Here you come with your Economics. If ever the Devil
designed
A science, 't was yours, I doubt not, a study to Hell's own
mind,
Merciless, soulless, sordid, the science of selfish greed, 10
Blind to the light of wisdom, and deaf to the voice of need.
And you prate of the wealth of nations, as if it were bought 15

and sold!
The wealth of nations is men, not silk and cotton and gold.
How will you measure in money the cost of knowledge and
Art?
Is honour valued in bank-notes? Can you pay for a broken
heart?
Can you reckon the worth of a poem by a standard of meat
and drink?
Can you buy with gold and silver a heart too great to
shrink?
Tell me, how many dollars will pay for the life-blood shed
From the veins of the true and valiant who feared not and
are dead?
Battle is fearful—I grant it. The fields are burnt bare with its
breath,   20
Death and the wrongs of women that cry out louder than
death,
The grime and the trampled faces and the shrieking of
shells in the air,
White lips of victims that pray and there comes no help for
their prayer,
And Famine that follows the armies, and Crime that skulks
in their rear,—
These are fearful alike to the soldiers that strike and the
cravens that fear.   25

But there's yet one woe far worse than war with its griefs
and graves—
To sink to a nation of cowards, sycophants, thieves and
slaves,
There is one thing for man or nation more within man's
control
And worse than the death of the body, and that is the death
of the soul.
But the sins of the city are silent and her ruin is wrought by
stealth   30
And the sores that fester are cloaked and her rottenness
masks as health.
True Peace is a holy thing—the peace God gives to his
own,
Heart's peace, though the body move where the thickest
shot is thrown,
Deeps of peace forever unplumbed by a mortal eye—
But the peace of the world is the Devil's, a mockery and a
lie,   35

Better city arrayed against city and hamlet with hamlet at
strife,
So valour outvalue lucre and honour be more than life.

A LYRIC

AND if some day he come back,
What should he be told?—
Tell him he was waited for,
Till my heart was cold.
And if he ask me yet again,   5
Not recognizing me?—
Speak him fair and sisterly;
His heart breaks, maybe.
And if he ask me where you are,
What shall I reply?—   10
Give him my golden ring,
And make no reply.
And if he ask me why the hall
Is left desolate?—
Show him the unlit lamp   15
And the open gate.
And if he should ask me, then,
How you fell asleep?—
Tell him that I smiled, for fear
Lest he should weep.   20

THE LOST COMRADE

NOW who will tell me aright
The way my lost companion went in the night?
My vanished comrade who passed from the roofs of men,
And will not come again.

I have wandered up and down   5
Through all the streets of this bright and busy town,
Yet no one has seen a trace of him since the day
He silently went away.

I have haunted the wharves and the slips,
And talked with foreigners from the incoming ships;   10
But when I questioned them closely about my friend,
They seemed not to comprehend.

From men of book-learning, too,   15

I have sought knowledge, confident that they knew;
But when I inquired simply about my chum,
They glanced at me and were dumb.

I have entered your churches of stone,
And heard discourse about God and the throng round his throne;
But the preacher knew nothing at all, when I broke in with, "Where?"
And the people could only stare.   20

Ah, no, you may read and read,
Pile modern heresy upon ancient creed!
But for all your study you know no more than I,
Under the open sky.

So 't is, Back to the Inn! for me,   25
Where my great friend and I were happy and free.
And I will remember his beautiful words and his ways,
For the rest of my days.

How eager he was for truth,
Yet never scorned the good things of his youth,   30
The soul of gentleness and the soul of love!
I shall be wise enough.

TEN COMMANDMENTS

It is right:

I. LOVE

TO love everybody a little and some people a great deal.

II. FAITH

To trust the God who made us is good and will not forget us.   5

III. OBEDIENCE

To obey those who have the right to hold themselves
responsible for us.

IV. HOPE

To look on the bright side of things and keep a good heart
up.

V. COURAGE   10

To dare do whatever we think we ought to do.

VI. CHEERFULNESS

To express our good, happy feelings, not the others.

VII. PRUDENCE

To use our intelligence to avoid trouble.   15

It is wrong:

VIII

To hate or hurt any one, except for a greater good; to be mean and selfish; to

        be unjust.

IX

To tell lies, except when people ask what they have no right to know.   20

X

To do anything dirty, or ugly, or intemperate.

QUATRAINS

LIFE as it is! Accept it; it is thine!
The God that gave it, gave it for thy good.
The God that made it had not been divine
Could he have set thee poison for thy food.

II

Abstain not; Life and Love, like night and day,   5
Offer themselves to us on their own terms,
—Not ours. Accept their bounty while ye may,
Before we be accepted by the worms.

III

We rail at Time and Chance, and break our hearts
To make the glory of to-day endure.   10
Is the sun dead because the day departs?
And are the suns of Life and Love less sure?

IV

Fear not the menace of the bye-and-bye.
To-day is ours; to-morrow Fate must give.
Stretch out your hands and eat, although ye die!   15
Better to die than never once to live.

THE ADVENTURERS

WE are the adventurers who come
Before the merchants and the priests;
Our only legacy from home,
A wisdom older than the East's.
Soldiers of Fortune, we unfurl   5
The banners of a forlorn hope,
Leaving the city smoke to curl
O'er dingy roofs where puppets mope.
We are the Ishmaelites of earth
Who at the crossroads beat the drum;   10
None guess our lineage nor our birth,
The flag we serve nor whence we come.
We claim a Sire that no man knows,
The Emperor of Night and Days,
Who saith to Caesar, "Go,"—he goes,   15
To Alexander, "Stay,"—he stays.
Out of a greater town than Tyre,
We march to conquer and control
The golden hill-lands of Desire,
The Nicaraguas of the soul.   20

We have cast in our lot with Truth;
We will not flinch nor stay the hand,
Till on the last skyline of youth
We look down on his fair new land.
We put from port without a fear,   25
For Freedom on this Spanish Main;
And the great wind that bore us here
Will drive our galleys home again.
If not, we can lie down and die,
Content to perish with our peers,   30
So one more rood we gained thereby
For Love's Dominion through the years.